DEC 2004

LT Fic
Blake,
Marriage materia

S0-AVS-708

WITHDRAWN

MARRIAGE MATERIAL

MARRIAGE MATERIAL

BY

ALLY BLAKE

MILLS & BOON®

ALAMEDA FREE LIBRARY
2200-A CENTRAL AVENUE
ALAMEDA, CA 94501

To Mum, who gave me my love of books, and Dad,
who couldn't wait to see what I would become.

All the characters in this book have no existence outside the imagination of the author, and have no relation whatsoever to anyone bearing the same name or names. They are not even distantly inspired by any individual known or unknown to the author, and all the incidents are pure invention.

All Rights Reserved including the right of reproduction in whole or in part in any form. This edition is published by arrangement with Harlequin Enterprises II B.V. The text of this publication or any part thereof may not be reproduced or transmitted in any form or by any means, electronic or mechanical, including photocopying, recording, storage in an information retrieval system, or otherwise, without the written permission of the publisher.

MILLS & BOON and
MILLS & BOON with the Rose Device
are registered trademarks of the publisher.

First published in Great Britain 2004
Large Print edition 2004
Harlequin Mills & Boon Limited,
Eton House, 18-24 Paradise Road,
Richmond, Surrey TW9 1SR

© Ally Blake 2004

ISBN 0 263 18113 8

Set in Times Roman 16 on 17¼ pt.
16-1004-51553

Printed and bound in Great Britain
by Antony Rowe Ltd, Chippenham, Wiltshire

PROLOGUE

'DELILAH! Don't you look just beautiful?' Sebastian raved to his favourite girl and earned a dimple-bright grin for his efforts.

Delilah had dressed herself in a dazzling ensemble of a rainbow-striped T-shirt, denim overalls, a pink frilly apron and yellow galoshes. Her curly blonde hair was decorated with a colourful assortment of ribbons and bobbles. Yet somehow on a four-year-old it worked.

She launched herself into his waiting arms and Sebastian whooped as though his niece had knocked the wind out of him. 'You may be beautiful but you are seriously heavy. Did you eat bricks for lunch?'

'No.'

'Elephants?'

'No!'

'Chocolate cake?'

She pulled back and her big brown eyes grew round with surprise. 'How could you tell?' she asked, her voice a sweet lisping whisper.

Sebastian squeezed her around the middle, tickling as he went. 'Yep, there it is, a chocolate-cake-shaped wedge.'

Delilah squirmed as she erupted into a fit of giggles.

'Aren't you supposed to be somewhere?' Delilah's mum, Melinda, chastised her younger brother, but her voice was warmed by gentle undertones.

Sebastian grimaced as he looked at his watch. 'There's no way I'm going to make it in time as it is, so another ten minutes can't hurt.'

Melinda's raised eyebrows showed how much she disagreed.

'Are you taking me to afternoon kindergarten, Unca Seb?' Delilah asked.

Sebastian looked to his sister for confirmation. She said nothing, just shoved her watch beneath his nose.

'I know, I know.' But Sebastian's priorities meant this particular appointment could wait. 'Would you like me to?'

'Do you have the big car?'

The big car was Sebastian's Jeep, plastic flap windows, roll bar, and abrasions streaking the once shiny black paintwork from much serious four-wheel driving. For some reason Delilah preferred this to his sleek sports car, which her older brothers favoured. She was going to be a spitfire, this one, no glamour puss, and Sebastian could not wait to see how she would turn out.

'Of course I have the big car. I knew I was coming to see you.'

'Then you can take me!'

Sebastian gathered her up and Melinda handed him Delilah's Barbie lunchbox and matching backpack.

'Bye, Ma!'

'Bye, munchkin.' Melinda gave Delilah a big smooch on the cheek.

'Bye, sis!' Sebastian stuck out his cheek for the same and received a fierce pinch instead.

He bundled his niece across the yard, through the frosty Melbourne winter air, and into his 'big car'. He snapped and tightened Delilah's seat belt and could not help but smile when he saw her feet only just reached the edge of the front seat.

She must have sensed his attention as she turned to him, her blonde curls bouncing about her ears, and cast him her sweetest smile.

His heart clenched. Once he dropped her off, the car would be empty, just like his spacious home, where for years numerous spare bedrooms had awaited the cheeky spirit and raucous giggles of children.

He gunned the engine, pumping the accelerator more than necessary but the noise helped obliterate the nagging sense of loneliness that had been creeping up on him all morning.

He glanced at the clock in the dashboard. He was fifteen minutes late already. He drove out onto the tree-lined suburban street. What did fifteen minutes matter when *no matter* what he did that day, by the time he got back home, it would be to a big, empty house once more?

CHAPTER ONE

FURIOUSLY caressing her favourite calming crystal, a smooth, misshapen ball of blue lace agate, Romy was able to keep her mounting impatience in check.

He's late, Romy thought, sending a calm, no-worries smile to the three others who sat with her around the modern kidney-shaped conference table. *Make that very late.*

They were all awaiting the arrival of Sebastian Fox, an ex-golf pro turned professional tomcat, a serial fiancé who nevertheless had walked the aisle to marriage but once, lasted six months at that, and, if all went according to Romy's plan, the soon-to-be ex-husband of her client.

Rather than do the impolite thing and release her frustration by screaming obscenities at the top of her lungs, Romy stood and walked to the doorway.

'Since we might be here a while yet,' Romy said, her voice the model of composure, 'who wants a cuppa?'

Gloria, Romy's legal assistant, dressed in her customary head-to-toe basic black, requested plain coffee, black also.

Janet, Romy's client, was irritable and very good at it. Even the ambient sound of waves lapping at a far-away beach pulsing from hidden speakers could not surmount the incessant tattoo of her long, painted fingernails rapping on the smooth Formica tabletop. She ordered a tall espresso, extra-strong, and Romy wondered whether the tabletop would survive her attentions once that level of caffeine hit her system.

Sebastian Fox's lawyer, Alan Campbell, who sat alone on the concave side of the table, seemed hypnotised by the drumming of Janet's fingernails. Apparently caffeine upset his stomach ulcer so he settled on a glass of water with which to take some Alka-Seltzer.

All three seemed on the verge of spontaneous combustion, such were their palpable jitters. Romy wondered it she ought to have offered each a nice cold cup of Prozac instead, or decaf in the least.

With her much-rubbed calming stone in hand, Romy wandered through the ultra-modern open-plan suite of legal offices of the boutique Archer Law Firm, in which she had worked the last five years, feeding off the optimistic energy the place exuded.

She waved hello to several clients who were not there for legal advice but for the numerous in-house programmes to help them get back on their feet post-divorce, such as cooking classes, single-parent counselling and even a new divorcee-dating scheme Romy had been instrumental in setting up.

With the usual spring in her step she made a beeline for the complimentary self-contained coffee hut by the lift.

'Good morning, Hank.' On tiptoe, Romy leaned over the counter to give the lovely elderly guy who ran the mobile café a kiss on the cheek.

'Well, it is now, Ms Bridgeport. Gloria did not come around for your usual this morning. I was worried you had called in sick.'

'Not at all. Healthy as could be. Vitamins every day are the trick.'

She put in her order and was content to keep half an ear on Hank as he happily chatted away about his favourite Australian Rules football team's mid-season winning streak.

To combat her left foot's growing desire to tap out her frustrations on the blond wood floor,

Romy rolled her stone around in her palm, soaking up every bit of positive energy she could. The blue lace agate was supposed to bestow clarity and would concentrate her self-expression, which she would need when the opposing client showed up, if he ever showed up.

The lift door pinged and Romy nonchalantly turned to see who had arrived. As though rubbing her crystal had raised a genie, Sebastian Fox had arrived dead on queue. And, like any respectable genie, he had brought forth a man who looked little like the grainy pictures Romy had in her legal dossier and more like he had stepped straight out of *GQ* magazine.

Well, at least he's finally here, she rationalised.

Romy's *rational* gaze raked over dark chestnut hair. Smooth, clear skin. A square face. Enviable sooty lashes that framed seductive grey-green eyes. His inviting mouth that appeared on the verge of a secret smile forced her spare hand to rest on her stomach to calm the wayward butterflies cavorting within. The reaction he invoked in her was instant, primal and unstoppable and all her conscientious crystal-rubbing went to waste in a heartbeat.

She had known men like him before. Men with strong tall frames, with broad shoulders, slim hips and muscular thighs, encased in cashmere and cargoes that highlighted every centimetre of glorious man flesh. But she had been there, done that, and burnt the T-shirt.

Romy continued to spin on her high heels as his eyes locked on to the quirky aqua desk at the end of the room where two cute guys and one cute girl sat below a big plastic downward-pointing arrow suspended from the ceiling above. As he passed Romy went to say something, to call out, to introduce herself, to yell at him for his serious lateness, but for a woman who made her living talking, she simply could not find the words.

Sure, she had known men on the high end of the hunk scale, but she had not known a stranger to smell that good! She caught the drifting scent of soap and cinnamon and felt an insistent physical tug like a dog on a lead, and was in very real fear that she was watching after him with her tongue hanging out.

Though it took her a few diverted moments to recall why she so detested him, she finally managed. The man who was leaning over the desk, causing both the girl *and* the guys at

Reception to go goo-goo-eyed, was no less than a physical affront to her whole belief system.

He was practically a professional groom-to-be, having been engaged to three women in seven years with very little time to himself in between. Janet had been the third, and she wondered momentarily what she had done differently that afforded her a wedding band to match the killer diamond on her left hand. But whatever it was in the end it still had not lasted.

And Romy was an anomaly in the field of divorce law. She was an advocate *for* marriage. She went to the nth degree to free her clients from bad marriages for the express purpose of giving them the opportunity to find true marital happiness elsewhere.

'Are you all right, Ms Bridgeport?' Hank asked, luring her attention back to the coffee hut.

'Sure, fine. And you?' She deserved the bemused blink Hank shot back.

'I'm fine,' he said. 'Your order is ready. I've added a plateful of Melting Moments.'

'Thanks, Hank.'

'You knock 'em dead, Ms Bridgeport.'

'With pleasure, Hank.'

Romy gathered the tray and turned around but Sebastian was gone. Into the conference room already, she assumed.

As she walked around the assortment of modern couches and avant-garde coffee-tables in the reception area, then through winding halls to the conference room, she hung on tight to her aversion to the man and to the tray heavy with scorching hot drinks and to the stone, which she now feared she would have to swallow to possess any real calming energy.

Two wrong turns sent Sebastian to a crèche and then to some sort of cooking class. If not for the smattering of suited men and women with yellow legal pads under their arms he would not have believed he was in a law firm. But even so, the promising impression of the place was fast overcome by more pressing matters. He knocked on the open door of the conference room and entered.

Alan stood and rushed over to him. 'About bloody time, mate.'

'Sorry. Events conspired to keep me anywhere but here.'

Alan laughed. 'Sure they did.'

A tap-tap-tap on a tabletop caught Sebastian's attention.

'I recognise that sound,' he said as he spun to face the source. It was Janet. And he also recognised what the tap-tap-tap meant. He walked around the table, took her hands, drew her to her feet and kissed her on the cheek.

'You're late,' she said.

'I got caught up with Delilah,' he told her. '*Had* to take her to afternoon kindergarten.' It was almost the truth.

'You and those kids. You spent more time with them than with me. You know that's why we are here today, don't you?'

He knew it to be true and it saddened him it had turned out that way. 'What can I say? I think I've proven I'm not husband material.'

He said it with a wry smile but the reality of the situation was no laughing matter. That empty feeling he had experienced dropping Delilah off at kindergarten had only grown as the day progressed.

Janet sighed in resignation. She laid a talon-tipped hand on his cheek. 'That's rubbish, darlin'. You're just not the husband for me.'

That brought on a smile. Despite the *misunderstanding* that had led him to believe she was the one for him, she was a good woman and more perceptive than she would have preferred to let on. But it was true, she was not the woman for him, no matter how, for their very different reasons, they had both tried to believe otherwise.

Janet lightly slapped his face before sitting down beside an intense young woman in head-to-toe black.

Sebastian had heard on the grapevine that Janet's lawyer was a ball-breaker, a man-hater, and this one certainly looked to fit that bill. With her dark clothing, her short dark hair waxed into sharp elfin spikes, and her large eyes lathered in lashings of mascara she was almost frightening. Almost.

The haughty letters he had received through Alan from the office of one Ms Bridgeport had conjured up images of a stuffy old spinster, grey-streaked hair raked back into a bun, navy suit buttoned up to the throat. But the angry-looking pixie before him looked as though she could out-haughty even the dowdiest spinster.

'Sebastian,' Alan said as though reading his mind, 'this is Gloria, Ms Bridgeport's assistant.'

Well, maybe he would be right yet. Since they were the only ones in the room, the grey-haired spinster was probably in her office, putting in her hourly phone call to her cats, and would be with them soon, smelling of mothballs and secretly imbibed rum. He smiled at the thought.

Romy reached the doorway and saw Sebastian's secret smile was now not so secret any more, and she was flummoxed afresh. She would have had to have lived in a cage not to have seen that smile shine from her TV screen numerous times over the last several years. Whether he had been holding up a golfing trophy or acting as spokesman for a children's charity, that free and easy grin had been enough for her channel-flicking finger to pause over the remote every time.

Romy watched in silence as Gloria found herself on the receiving end of such a smile.

'Gloria,' Sebastian said and his voice was deep and tempting and complemented all the other delectable bits of him. 'It's a pleasure to meet you.'

But Gloria, bless her little heart, radiated resplendent disapproval. What a trooper. She gave Sebastian's hand a perfunctory shake before letting go and wringing her hands together, erasing any sign of their contact. Romy had to stifle a laugh.

Alan caught Romy's eye and she knew the time had come to meet the enemy. Gloria spied her at the same time and hurried to hand out the order of drinks.

'Romy Bridgeport,' Alan said, 'this is my client, Sebastian Fox.'

She squared her shoulders, smoothed out her dress, and battened down the hatches. *He is nothing but a heartless cad,* she reminded herself, *and you are going to take him down!*

And as the man in question turned to face her a pair of three-foot-high twin boys bundled into the room, screaming, 'Womy! Womy!' in falsetto unison.

They leapt at her legs, clinging tight like limpets. Romy's smoothed-out dress rode high up her thighs as her legs split shoulder-width apart in order for her to just about keep her balance. It was hardly the stern and intimidating impression she had been hoping to strike!

Whatever Sebastian had been expecting it had not been her. She was no grey-haired spinster, she was no angry pixie, and she was like no lawyer he had ever seen.

Romy Bridgeport was tall and slender as a reed in a form-hugging sea-blue dress that at that moment was hiked halfway up her cover-girl thighs. A matching jacket that looked as though it would considerably cover the slip of a garment was currently not earning its keep as it hung casually over the back of her chair.

But what hit him most was her mane of glowing auburn hair. It was long, lush and healthy and cut with a flirty fringe. With her china-blue eyes and lithe grace she looked more like a mermaid than a lawyer.

And while she laughed and bashfully enjoyed every second of the young boys' company, Alan yawned, Gloria was hot on the phone, probably calling for their minders, and Janet was all but crouched on her chair as though the room had been overrun by mice. No surprise there. Not any more. Sebastian had too late discovered Janet was not a kid person on the day she had inadvertently admitted that previously unavowed truth in the same way one would say one was not a cat person.

'Hey, kiddos,' Romy said, her voice breathy, 'how did you find me? Where is Samantha?'

'Womy, wead a stowy!' one of them demanded as only three-year-olds could.

She shot an apologetic look that encompassed the whole group, her blue eyes glittering in a mixture of delight and mortification. 'Romy is busy right now. She is reading these fine people a story for the next little while.'

'What stowy?' the other cherub asked.

And without missing a beat she said, 'It's a story where Rapunzel takes on the mean troll...and wins.'

Sebastian had to fight back a laugh.

'But we don't want Rapunzel to win.'

Hey! Boys after his own heart!

'I figured as much,' Romy said. 'So how about you guys head back to Samantha's room and I will come over later and tell you the story of when the mean troll and his even meaner cousin, the ogre, ate Rapunzel? OK?'

The boys stopped squirming and through some sort of telepathic twin communication they let go and ran off as fast as they had appeared, their excited squeals echoing down the hall.

'My apologies,' she said to the group, 'they belong to one of the partners and have taken quite a fancy to my more gory tales.'

'I don't blame them,' Sebastian admitted. 'The troll *and* the ogre. Sounds too good to miss.'

But when her derisive china-blue gaze clashed with his, the smile fast disappeared. An adorable blush lit her pale cheeks as she straightened her dress, and tidied her now magnificently messy hair.

He reached out to shake her hand across the table, enjoying the way the fabric of her almost dress clung to her thighs as, after a distinct pause, she bent towards him. Her hand was cool and soft and felt small in his own. 'Ms Bridgeport. So glad to finally meet you face to face.'

'I'm just glad you could *finally* find the time, Mr Fox.' Her pleasant voice held a strong thrust of steel beneath the airy sound.

'Sebastian, please,' he offered.

She gave him a slight nod, though did not return the offer to use her own first name.

Her face was a mask of disinterested civility, but he didn't buy it for a second. Though she was trying so hard to appear serene and in control she was bristling with kinetic energy. Most lawyers he had come across were stale and tired to say the least but she was so dynamic it was infectious. He could barely stand still himself. And compared with the lassitude that had threatened to overwhelm him only moments before, it was a blessing.

'Romy, was it?' he said, not giving up. 'Interesting name. I bet there is a great story behind that one.'

She bit into a biscuit rather than on to his line and he caught sight of a row of very short and faintly ragged fingernails. Hmm. So she was a nail-biter and *not* so much the tough cookie as she behaved.

'There are more important things to discuss today than my name, Mr Fox,' Romy said. 'Go ahead, take a seat so we can focus our energies where they belong.'

Fair enough. He did as he was told and slumped back into his seat, his expression all seriousness to show her he was ready to deal with the task at hand. But she had also taken a seat and her attention had left him without a second thought. She was running a hand through her hair until it settled in a lustrous ripple down her back, and, casually crossing one long leg over the other, she showcased an expanse of one lovely, creamy thigh.

Whoa.

Romy shifted uncomfortably in her seat. She was surprised to find that her opposition seemed to be almost enjoying himself! And Romy hated surprises. They were never positive. Ever. If you knew what was coming you could cope, no matter how big a deal. But the not knowing was a killer.

No, she determined. There would be no surprises. It would all be fine. She was ready. She'd spent every minute of her adult life making sure she would be ready for any situation, so she was *not* in the least bit nervous. Well, not much anyway.

'Mr Campbell, *Mr Fox,* let's get this over and done with, shall we? Then we can all get on with more pleasant pursuits.'

Sebastian turned a leisurely glance her way and the pleasant pursuits that filled her head sent her heart thumping against her ribs as her adrenalin kicked in full force.

Bad. Bad Romy!

She grabbed her calming stone and put it to better use as a paperweight. Energy flow and inner beauty could wait. By cornering her, the tomcat had released a hellcat who would very soon be wiping that all too free and easy smile from his face.

'Mr Fox,' she began, 'I think my client has the right to a great deal larger settlement than you have suggested and here is a small selection of the innumerable irrefutable reasons why…'

In an hour it was all over.

Before Romy had even hit her stride in her savage roast, Sebastian capitulated.

He glanced at his watch, said, 'Sorry to cut the game short, guys. It's been a blast but I have a date. Give Janet whatever she wants.'

Now, that was one heck of a surprise! As, although the guy was a renowned playboy who had left behind a daisy chain of well-kept women who had kindly kept him company on those long, cold Melbourne nights, he had never even suggested a pre-nuptial agreement before marrying. So Janet getting what she wanted was a fair whack.

Sebastian grabbed a pen from the table, signed Romy's contracts with a flourish, patted his lawyer on the back and left without a backward glance.

He had given up an exorbitant amount of money so as not to break a *date*. For a guy who seemed to go through women as if they were going out of fashion, Romy couldn't help but wonder who could be that important to him.

And in some small, ridiculous part of Romy's anatomy, she felt a pang of something akin to envy towards someone who could mean that much in Sebastian Fox's life.

CHAPTER TWO

AN HOUR later Sebastian was still trying to push the thought of the lawyer and her stinging criticism from his mind.

A thin, high voice called out from across the oval. 'Hey, Seb. Heads up!'

Sebastian scooped the ball up and weaved in and out of the group of youngsters running at his side, relishing the heat and sweat and opportunity to exercise away the niggling frustration that had tagged him all day. He eventually slowed enough for his elder nephew to tag him but not enough to make it look as if he wasn't trying.

'Tagged!' Chris called out in glee.

'Aah, you got me there, Chris.' Sebastian shook his head in disbelief as he handed over the football to his opposition. 'You're just too quick for an old man like me.'

Chris grinned proudly and yanked the ball from Sebastian's hands.

'Everybody ready?' Chris called out to the group straggling across the football field before taking off towards the goals.

A madly waving hand on the end of an adult arm on the sideline caught Sebastian's attention. He looked up-field and made sure another couple of adults were keeping control of the game before he jogged off the oval.

'Good to see you, Tom.' He gave his brother-in-law a bear hug.

'Hey, watch the threads. You're sweating all over me.'

Sebastian made sure to wipe his hands vigorously on the back of Tom's clean shirt before pulling away.

'You're getting thrashed out there, mate.'

Sebastian grinned. 'You think you can do better? You join us.'

Tom held up his palms in defeat. 'No, thanks. I've got this bad knee, remember.'

Sebastian raised his eyebrows in disbelief. 'Melinda told me all about that. Didn't you walk into the coffee-table? Three weeks ago?'

'That table has a really sharp corner.'

'Fine.' Sebastian turned and watched Chris weaving across the field, the ball in his possession again. 'You're just lucky you've got me around to make sure your kids get the exercise they need.'

'Sure, mate. Sure. Hey, Melinda told me today was D-day. Divorce day, right?'

'Yep.' The easy smile swiftly melted from Sebastian's face. He kicked at a tuft of grass on the edge of the field.

'So what did she get?' Tom grabbed Sebastian by the arm, the slick sweat coating him suddenly of no importance. 'You'd better not have given her the beach house. Melinda and I promised the kids a week there this summer.'

'She would never have even asked for the beach house.'

Tom's raised eyebrows showed he disagreed. 'I think you proved you were the last one to know what Janet might or might not do to get what she wants.'

Sebastian shrugged. 'Anyway, she got plenty.'

Tom let loose with a great laugh. 'For a girl who seemed easy come, easy go, she sure turned out to have a killer streak.'

'So we now know. But this wasn't Janet. This was the lawyer.'

The lawyer. So much for pushing her to the back of his mind. The instant action replay running constantly through his mind all afternoon, and frustrating him to distraction, had been all about the lawyer. Long legs, startling eyes, and that hair. And most of all the cutting accusations about his lifestyle she had flung at him with such vigour. He'd been brandished a playboy before. And even a cad. And maybe with good reason. But the lawyer had labelled him 'a neurotic caveman for whom women were merely bandages for his over-inflated ego'. And that had been rough.

'Must have been a real hot-shot,' Tom said, thankfully drawing Sebastian back to the comparative comfort of his current surrounds. 'What's his name?'

'*Her* name is Romy Bridgeport.'

Tom stopped laughing though his grin went from full-screen to wide-screen. 'You poor fellow. A couple of guys at work have been on the losing end of her counsel. But I thought if any guy had a chance against her charms it would have been you. She must be really something. Was she the man-hater I heard she is?'

'Well, I don't think she liked *me* much.'

'No? But I thought they *all* liked you, what with you being so cute and all.'

Tom reached out and gave Sebastian's cheeks a rough pinch. Sebastian playfully slapped his hands away. But he did not feel so playful.

It was true. She had not liked him one bit. She had not even tried to hide the fact for civility's sake. Yet despite it all he had been patently attracted to her. Attracted physically went without saying, but it was her vitality that kept him engaged even after she let fly with her unremitting accusations.

'Apparently she is engaged to some American,' Tom said, again dragging Sebastian back to the present. 'How ironic—a divorce lawyer getting married. You'd think she would be cynical about the whole deal.'

Sebastian did not remember seeing a sparkling diamond. But he had been blindsided by the significance behind the adorably short fingernails, so maybe… 'Engaged to an American, you say?'

'Mmm. Thing is, from what I've heard nobody has ever seen the guy or if they have they are keeping quiet about it. Maybe it's all a diversionary tactic to fend off hot-from-the-oven divorcees. *Don't even think about it, I'm engaged.*'

Sebastian looked up as a yell of glory erupted from the other end of the field. One of his team had scored a try. He looked back to Tom and shuffled from one foot to the other, itching to get back to the game.

'Saved by the yell,' Tom said. 'Go on, then. Get back out there. But I want details. Come for dinner and stay over tonight?'

'Fine,' Sebastian conceded as he ran backwards onto the field. 'Tell Melinda I'll be there at seven.'

Romy stumbled into her apartment-building foyer after ten o'clock. She had spent the evening with her divorced-singles group, with once battered wives, with cheated-on husbands, with a woman she had comforted in a quiet corner, and with a pair who had the amazing news that they had become engaged…to one another! They were serious people looking for serious relationships, and if Romy knew anything about anything, she knew about that.

She shuffled into the antiquated lift, pulled the doors shut and endured the interminable ride to her top-floor apartment. Rhythmic creaks and groans took the place of the electronic music you would find in most modern apartment-building lifts. In an atypical fit of whimsy she had picked the apartment for the beautiful restored lift with its open-cage design, and she'd had to endure its resultant slowness and periodic breakdowns ever since. That would teach her!

Once home she checked her answering machine. Her parents had sent their weekly 'hello' in duet. She could not remember the last time she had spoken to one and not the other. They were the most devoted couple she had ever come across, still deeply in love after thirty perfect years.

She called them back, and hooked the phone beneath her chin as she prepared herself a light snack.

'Hey, Mum.'

'Hey, baby. I saw you on TV tonight. The Press conference. With that lovely Janet Hockley. Will she continue to make those aerobic videos, do you think?'

Romy chomped on a celery stick. 'She made them before her marriage and during her marriage so I wouldn't think she would suddenly stop now.'

'Oh, good. I was thinking of buying the next one for your father for Christmas. It seems he doesn't mind the exercise so long as there's a cute young thing to show him how to do it. And I've hit the point that I'm willing to let him do anything so long as his cholesterol comes down.'

Romy set up her picnic on the small round table by the kitchen.

'And did you get to meet that husband of hers?'

'I did.'

'And was he the stud the magazines say he is?'

Her mind wandered to the image of him walking from office to lift. Throughout the day it had transformed into slow motion and sepia. Now her mother had unfortunately relocated that image to Sebastian walking through a stable, rake in hand, shining with sweat… She fought the urge to dislodge the looped vision from her mind with a sharp slap across the cheek.

'Not that I witnessed first-hand.'

Her mother paused and Romy hoped she did not pick up on the forced nonchalance in her voice. That was all she needed for her mother to get funny ideas in her head. Luckily her indifference seemed to fly.

'Well, I guess that's hardly something you could add to your résumé, dear, so no loss there.'

'True. Is Dad there?'

'He's on the other phone, listening, dear.'

Of course he was. 'All's well, Dad?'

'Well as can be expected considering your mother won't let me eat potato any more. Potato, I tell you!'

'Imagine if you got on her bad side. You'd be left with bread and water.'

'Bread! Ha! She made me cut out bread long before potato became the evil food of the month—'

'Anyway,' Romy's mother cut him off, 'we just wanted to say we saw you on TV, dear. The girls at poker will be most impressed. Goodnight, love.'

'Goodnight, Mum. 'Night, Dad.'

Romy hung up, appalled as the slow-motion, sepia, gorgeous-man-walking image was now replaced with the hazy image of Sebastian, the stud, dripping in hay and little else.

No! She was not a woman willing to have her head turned by an enchanting smile. She was stronger than that, more focused, and with very specific plans for her future, and mooning over a man *like him* did not come into that equation.

Romy was confident that like her parents she would never, ever marry unless she was sure it would be forever. Whereas this guy went through wives the way he went through baseball caps. Lucky he was Alan's client, not hers, so it was unlikely she would run into him ever again.

She felt very sorry for the next Mrs Sebastian Fox. Whoever she was.

Sebastian walked into the kitchen early the next morning with his sister's middle child Thomas slung squealing and twisting over his shoulder.

'Put me down, Uncle Sebastian! You promised as soon as we got to the kitchen table!'

'I promised once you finished my maths quiz. Come on, Thomas. Five times five is…'

Thomas took a deep, uncertain breath. 'Twenty-five?'

'That's my boy.' Sebastian tickled his nephew until tears welled in his eyes.

'Put him down, Sebastian, or I'll never get him to school.' Melinda mixed several eggs in the frying pan and slopped in some milk and cheese.

'Yes, sis.' Sebastian swung the boy from his shoulders and plopped him at the kitchen bench next to Chris and Delilah.

'You should be cooking for me,' Melinda said. 'I have to get ready for work. What are you doing today?'

'Don't know.'

'When are you going to get a real job, Uncle Sebastian?' Thomas asked.

Melinda grinned. 'From the mouths of babes...'

Sebastian ruffled his nephew's hair, earning a squeal of torment for his efforts. 'I do just fine, thank you very much.'

'It's not about doing fine. It's about using your gifts for good.'

He pushed Melinda aside with a bump of his hip and finished making the eggs for her. She set to getting the kids ready for school.

'With my sponsorships and investments, I'm building a pretty meaty trust fund for your young tribe, sis, so I'm hardly using them for evil.'

Melinda was unmoved. 'You hardly use them at all. If not a job then a hobby other than babysitting or playing touch footy and marrying badly. You need a project. I can't stand watching you atrophy before my eyes.'

He chose to ignore Melinda's barb. Though it had been playing on him all night. A project?

Was that what he needed? He felt he was on the verge of something. As if he just needed a nudge and a truth would be revealed. He had no idea what it was but he felt invigorated, more than he had in years.

Sebastian lifted his shirt to reveal a very healthy torso. 'What do you reckon, kids? Still enough to keep me going for a few winters yet?' He poked his tummy out as far as it would go and scored a giggle from his nephews.

Melinda was about to hit him when Tom, senior, shouted out from the den. 'That's her!'

'I've asked him a thousand times not to shout if he wants me, but to come and get me,' Melinda said to Sebastian, her voice rising until it was more than a match for her husband's. 'He sets the kids such a bad example!'

'It's the lawyer!' Tom shouted once more. 'The one who took Sebastian to the cleaners yesterday.'

That caught Sebastian's attention. He pulled down his shirt and hotfooted it into the den, where he sat on the arm of Tom's couch. It was a Press conference from the day before. Romy's sea-blue suit jacket was buttoned up to the neck no less, but nothing bar a big woollen hat could hide that shock of magnificent hair.

Tom whistled long and slow. 'And boy, is she a babe!'

And then some, Sebastian thought, feeling his breathing slow perceptibly at the sight of her. But now he saw the danger signs as they appeared. What he was feeling was precisely the pattern Romy had reiterated he had followed all his adult life. That for whatever reason, he fell into one set of female arms after another. So according to her theories his attraction to her would simply be because she was in the line of fire.

'Who's a babe?' Melinda asked from the doorway.

'You are, my love.'

Tom grinned and patted his lap. Melinda rolled her eyes but followed his instructions and snuggled onto his lap anyway. Sebastian saw this interplay only from the corner of his eye as his gaze was focused on the tabloid TV show in front of him.

'*That* was your opposition lawyer,' Melinda said. Then she too laughed. 'I would have put money on the outcome to go *her* way. I'll give it to Janet—despite her foibles, she is a clever, clever girl.'

Sebastian had had a feeling from the moment he'd walked in that room that Janet was a *lucky, lucky* girl. The clever one had been sitting beside her, pulling all the strings. More importantly, that clever one was someone who knew what she wanted and let nothing stand in her way. That certainty was what he had been missing. He'd had it once before time and life had whittled it away.

'You were right, bro. She doesn't like you much,' Tom said. 'You can see it in her eyes as clear as if she had said the words. She is as happy to have beaten you as she is that her client won.'

Melinda leant forward to get a closer look then turned to her brother with her mouth turned upside-down. 'Poor Sebastian. The one woman who won't be signing up to your fan club and she just happens to be on the opposing side of your divorce suit.'

Sebastian nodded but his mind was a long way further down the track. The room the Press conference was being held in looked familiar. Where had he seen it before? The cooking class! He had accidentally stumbled in there when searching for the conference room.

'They have quite some set-up down there, you know.'

'Do they, now?' He felt rather than saw Melinda give Tom a look.

'They have a crèche, a café, cooking classes for the newly single.'

The feeling that had been building up in him all morning hit some sort of crescendo then spilled over into understanding. He suddenly knew what he was going to do that day.

'I was thinking of going back there to check it out further.'

'You want to take a cooking class?'

Sebastian peeled himself from the chair; he felt as if he was waking up after a long sleep. 'Maybe. Why not?'

'Why not, indeed?' Melinda agreed. 'Maybe you should go back and check *it* out.'

'Maybe I will.'

But he knew that there was no maybe about it.

Romy walked back from her early-morning Pilates class to her office in her gym outfit of a snug tank top, ankle-length gym tights and white sneakers, whistling a tune she had heard in the cab radio on the way to work. The towel wrapped around her neck kept lank hair off her hot skin.

Once in her office she slid the towel from beneath her hair, performed a pretty spectacular butt-wiggle in time with the conclusion of the jazzy song, and threw her towel over her shoulder towards her sofa. She stopped short, as she did not hear the usual soft slap of towel hitting seat.

'Mornin', Romy,' a deep, sexy voice called to her.

She spun around, her hand smothering the scream that escaped her throat, and found Sebastian Fox leaning back in her sofa, the old towel clutched in his hand. She had to resist the substantial urge to whack him for giving her such a shock.

'According to your day planner you should have been back,' he looked at his watch, 'three minutes and twenty seconds ago. I was getting worried.'

'You read my diary?' she blurted.

'I couldn't miss it. It is open on your desk and takes up almost as much space. I've never met anyone who diarised what they are going to wear for the next week!'

'Dry cleaning efficiently is a finicky business. And so what if I am organized? What's wrong with that?'

Romy had to shake her head to remember how this conversation had even begun.

'I think the pertinent information is what on earth you are doing here, Mr Fox. I can assure you the contract you signed was legal and binding, therefore you have no recourse to insist on any changes.'

Sebastian stilled. He had caught sight of the Barbie insignia emblazoned across the length of Romy's towel. The smile he shot her was enquiring and…*impressed*?

'It's the smallest clean towel I could find at home this morning,' she waffled.

Sebastian nodded as though her explanation made it seem less ridiculous, then she was forced to wait as he neatly folded her towel and placed it on the seat beside him. As such she was also forced to notice how unfairly scrumptious he looked in his black sweater. His hair was mussed from the wind outside and light stubble covered his swarthy cheeks and chin. His stormy eyes gleamed in the low morning light and he looked far too alert for so early in the day.

He caught her watching him and smiled again, this time it was slow and languorous and she felt it in her gut. Of course, that was probably hunger from not having had breakfast before her class.

'I thought maybe we could talk shop.' His smile lit up with mischief. 'Though perhaps I have caught you at a bad time.'

'Because I am dressed as such?' she asked, waving a frustrated hand down the length of her insufficiently clad body. 'Goodness no. It's Wednesday. We all go ultra-casual on a Wednesday.'

But it was not her skimpy outfit that bothered her as such. It was that the day before at least she had been prepared for the sensory onslaught that was he. She had been Ms Bridgeport the lawyer, and her attire, her props, had all been a part of the magic act and she had felt right at home on the stage she had set. Right now she was still numb with surprise and not ready for the likes of him. She was Romy the sleepy, Romy the sweaty, Romy of the Barbie towel.

It was time to regain her home-court advantage. She walked around her desk and sat in her office chair, happier to have a huge obstacle between herself and his keen gaze. She casually picked up her heavy blue crystal and rolled it around in her palm.

'Since your ex-wife is a client of mine I'm not sure how much shop we can talk without ethics getting in the way. Though I'm not sure that would have occurred to *you*.'

There, Romy thought, *take that*!

'Actually that did occur to me. So I rang Janet this morning and she assured me her contract with you was finalised as soon as I signed on the dotted line.'

How chummy. Even his ex-wife was on phone-chatting terms. Well, she was not falling for the all-too-cool façade. She knew better than anyone that an angelic face did not an angel make.

'Fine. You want to talk shop, Mr Fox, then talk shop.'

'I think this place is pretty amazing.'

Well, she couldn't argue with that. 'Go on.'

'And of all the amazing sights I witnessed yesterday you are the cream on the cake. You are a force to be reckoned with, Romy. The best I have ever come up against.'

The way Sebastian said it made Romy imagine coming up against him in a whole different way than he had implied, and the mental picture raised her heart rate to twice the speed the Pilates had. There was no harm in blaming hunger *and* exercise-induced endorphins, was there?

'And I would like to secure your services,' he finished.

'That's very flattering, but if you are seeking my representation I am afraid that I am a specialist and I would be no use to you unless...'

Sebastian watched in amazement as the colour drained from Romy's face, making her startling eyes rimmed with smudged eyeliner stand out even more.

'Oh, no,' she said. 'Please don't tell me you already have another poor fish on your hook and you are already preparing for the time you will throw her back.'

Her statement was so ridiculous Sebastian almost laughed. But then he realised she was deadly serious. Her hand clamped tight onto a strange blue stone and he could swear she was on the verge of throwing it at him!

'There is no fish to speak of, Romy,' Sebastian said, simply unable to resist pandering to her self-righteousness. He wanted her up and fighting if he was going to get what he needed from her. 'But I am a pragmatic man and time is awaiting, as is the next ex-Mrs Sebastian Fox. She's out there somewhere and here we are, wasting time arguing about it, rather than giving the girl the chance to have a go.'

The nerve of the man! Romy's palms began to itch as the hot blood rushed to her edgy extremities. She lowered her crystal into her desk drawer to stop herself from pegging it between his eyes.

'I will not be your divorce lawyer, Mr Fox.' Her voice all but quivered with indignation.

'Once again, it's Sebastian.'

She took a deep breath and counted to three. 'Fine, then. I will not be your divorce lawyer, *Sebastian*. I act only for those who take marriage seriously and you, *Sebastian*, do not come across to me as a terribly serious person. And if you have really done your research you will know that I consider myself not in the business of promoting divorce but in the business of making sure the right people are together.'

'Fine.'

'Fine?'

'As I said, there is no fish to speak of. Not yet. So, since you are such a renowned matchmaker, I need you to assist me in procuring my next wife.'

CHAPTER THREE

'I THINK the best thing for me is to get back on the horse,' Sebastian said.

Romy's mouth hung ajar and her eyes were round and bright as dollar coins. 'Get…back…on…the…horse?'

Her face was crimson and absolutely delightful. He'd heard of women who were beautiful when they were angry but had thought it just a myth. But here was one woman for whom the saying could have been written.

'OK. So that was a bad analogy. Though you obviously don't see it *yet*, I will make someone a good husband,' he said, taking to the plan the more he fumbled his way through it. 'And, as you are a self-professed expert on the subject—'

'I am nothing so worthy as an expert, Mr Fox.'

'But you yourself are engaged, are you not?' he asked.

Her mouth snapped shut like a threatened clam and surprise flickered across her vibrant eyes. But she neither agreed nor denied the claim. He wondered if Tom was right and it was a fallacy she had created as a *hands-off* signal.

A cute young thing like her, spending every day with newly single male clients would surely have an excuse to create such a rumour. But Sebastian decided it was more likely the truth. Half the reason he fancied she was perfect for the job was the likelihood she was taken. It meant he had a good reason not to fall into the trap of seeing her as someone to ease his loneliness short-term when he needed to refocus on the big picture.

The steady disapproval in her magnetic blue eyes was unmistakable. But welcome. It was exactly that spirit that he needed to tap. And all the better that her heat remain directed against him not toward him. She was spoken for *and* she didn't much like him. Perfect.

'I've rung around and heard good things about your divorcees group,' he said.

'Mr Fox, I assure you there is no way that I am going to launch *you* upon that unassuming group of people. They are serious and they are damaged, whereas you…you act as if it is all just a game!'

Aah, so that was why she was so offended; she did not get to be the shoulder to cry on. She did not get to be the fix-it woman. Well, if that was what she needed to be…

'I assure you, Romy, it was no game. I am serious. I am damaged.' He held out his arms and even gave her his best go at a pout. She glared at him in disbelief but he thought he saw the first real flicker of interest.

With visible effort her face relaxed. Her tongue shot out to briefly wet her lips and she managed a fragile smile. 'I would not even know where to begin.'

'Well, that's the beauty. I'm a not only a willing and able participant but I also have a bevy of ideas. I just need your help to implement them. Besides, I am very certain you have researched my background so thoroughly you now know more about me than I do. So mould me. Shape me. Make me the kind of man any good woman would want to marry.'

Her eyes positively glowed and he knew it had nothing to do with recent exercise. She was once more lit with that inner fire, that spirit that so caught at him. He had finally found the right button to push to bring her on to his side. She was intrigued despite herself.

'I've done some homework and have heard about how *hands-on* your clients expect you to be. And I want that from you.'

Sebastian knew from the firm line of Romy's mouth the only hands-on approach she would be willing to give him right then was a right hook.

'I can't do it. I have other clients counting on me.'

'For the moment they can count on someone else.'

'I can refuse you as a client.'

'I will bring so much work your firm's way you will not have a choice.'

He stood, stretching like a sleepy cat, knowing it would only rile her more, and the fists clenching on her desk showed him it worked. 'Well, I'll leave you to prepare my file.'

'Don't count on it.'

He glanced over her barely dressed form and, since he was way beyond right-hook distance, he could not stop himself from saying, 'I'll see more of you soon.'

Then he left.

Once outside the city building, Sebastian took a deep breath of the still foggy morning air. But the grey sky could not dampen his mood. She was such a spitfire, yet so certain. If he had any chance of finding his footing again it would be at her side.

He couldn't believe that only the day before, after years of knowing he wanted a family of his own more than anything, his experience with Janet had made him think he had hit a point when it really might not happen for him. He saw the future on the horizon, shimmering like a mirage, but he knew it was real and just waiting for the right moment to slip into focus.

He took off up the street, whistling and smiling at strangers. One of those strangers turned out to be a familiar dark-haired pixie.

'Gloria! Good morning!'

She glared at him, her big eyes narrowing to slits as her perceptive gaze slid past him to her building beyond. 'Mr Fox. What brings you to this part of town?'

No point in pretending. She would know soon enough. 'I had a proposition to put forward that could not be refused.'

'And what was that?'

'Your boss is going to make a husband out of me.'

Gloria's eyebrows raised a good inch. 'Meaning?'

'Meaning, since she turns out to be not just a divorce perpetrator but also a marriage aficionado, I have signed on for her to teach me what being a good husband means, so that I will be ready when I meet the woman of my dreams.'

'Well, well, well. *That* I didn't see coming.'

'Unique, don't you agree?'

Gloria's mouth twitched. 'So *unique* that if I have a bad day at work today I'll know who to blame.'

Sebastian burst out laughing. 'Yet still I am not deterred. I made a good decision this morning, a decision to change my life, and I am sticking by it.'

'Then good for you.' Was that a smile that finally tickled at the corner of her mouth?

'If it turns out that my decision has... consequences, I'll make it up to you. What do you want? A case of wine? Wrestling tickets? My head on a stick? What would it take to have you on my side?'

The smile was finally in place. No teeth but definite lifts to the corners of her mouth. 'You want me on your side?'

Sebastian nodded. He had the distinct feeling Gloria could make it difficult for him otherwise.

'Then be on Romy's side,' Gloria said, melting enough to give him a chummy pat on the arm before she headed to work. And Sebastian watched her go with the feeling she may have been on to something even more inspired than he.

By the time Gloria arrived for work Romy had showered and changed into a much more appropriate little black dress with killer stiletto mules and had worked herself up into a right temper. She paced back and forth as Gloria took pages of notes about the meetings they would hold that day.

'When's my first appointment?' Romy asked.

'She's here. Mrs Libby Gold. She's fresh meat so be gentle. She looks nervous as an ant at an anteater convention.' Gloria drew a broad concluding line under her notes. 'You had Pilates this morning, did you not?'

'I did.'

'Aren't you taking the classes for stress release?'

'I am.'

'And do you think you are getting your money's worth?'

Romy stopped pacing and turned to her assistant, who was staring cross-eyed at portions of her short, spiky fringe which she was systematically pinching between her fingertips.

Romy sat deliberately on the corner of her desk and clasped her taut hands together in her lap. 'I had a visitor after class who undid all the instructor's fine work.'

'That doesn't seem fair. Maybe you should get Mr Fox to reimburse you.'

Romy could do nothing but stare. 'Well, maybe I should. What he suggested was just plain ridiculous.'

'I thought the makeover idea was whacko at first but it has kind of grown on me.'

Romy blinked. 'Nothing gets by you does it, Gloria?'

'Not a thing. And for that you should be thankful. But you will do it anyway, won't you?' Gloria asked.

'Of course I darned well will. He practically dared me and you know I can't refuse a challenge.'

And the guy was a clean slate. Malleable. If she could find Sebastian Fox, of all men, a woman with whom he would really settle down then it would prove that marriage could still work today. What a coup that would be.

And what an affirmation.

'Though how you noticed his challenge when that fine butt of his was walking by I have no idea.'

This coming from the woman who the previous week had told all and sundry that all men were chief purveyors of low self-esteem in women. 'I can't believe you noticed his butt when that fine ego of his was walking by.'

Gloria shrugged. 'Maybe there's more to him than the dossier suggested.'

'You do realise you are talking about a man, do you not?'

'And what a man—'

Romy pointed to her office door. 'Out.'

Gloria peeled her diminutive frame from the large chair. 'Yes, ma'am.'

Romy shot one more look at her clock. 'Send in Libby Gold and then as soon as she's gone patch me through to Alan Campbell.'

Gloria turned at the door and shot Romy a cheeky grin. 'Mr Fox's lawyer?'

'He just so happens to be.'

Gloria winked. 'Shall do, boss.'

Romy spent the next fifty minutes with Libby Gold, who for fifteen years had been the wife of a man who had made a fortune in toothpaste. She was sweet, she was matronly and she had no idea how she had found herself in a lawyer's office talking divorce.

Privately Romy was glad Libby had come to her as she knew she would take extra-special care of her. Taking her through the process slowly and surely. And taking her philandering husband to the cleaners.

'But what does that make the last fifteen years of my life?' Libby asked. 'A waste? I cannot handle the thought.'

'You can handle it, Libby, because it has not been a waste. It has been a grand lesson. For you both. He will pay for his mistake and you will come out of it with knowledge and experience and a tidy fortune to tide you over.'

'What good is money if I don't have Jeffrey? I can't bake a favourite meal for money. I can't rest my head on money's shoulder while watching a movie. People are what counts. People are what makes your life a life. Money has no memory.'

What could Romy say to that? The poor woman's mind was settled, for today anyway. Romy would win her around to the knowledge that the future was out there for the taking. That the man for her was still out there. And Romy had not lost a client back to their spouse once. Not ever. And she was not willing to start now.

Romy stood and patted her client on the shoulder. 'See Gloria on your way out and she'll tee you up for our next session.'

Once Libby was gone, Romy buzzed Gloria's intercom. 'Can you get Alan for me, Gloria?'

'I don't think now's the right time,' her voice mumbled through the black box on Romy's desk. 'We've had quite a spate of correspondence since you've been busy.'

She nibbled at a little fingernail. 'Well, are you going to tell me what the correspondence says?'

'Oh. Sure.'

Romy heard the squeak of Gloria's chair and she ambled into the office with a fresh cup of chamomile tea and bundle of faxes in her hands.

'What have you got there, my sweet?' Romy asked.

'Faxes.'

Romy took a deep calming breath. 'Saying?'

'The first came from Alan saying Mr Golf Pro has ceased services with his firm and to send any further correspondence to his new firm. And confirming usual drinks tonight at Fables?' Gloria looked up with questioning eyebrows.

Romy nodded vigorously. 'Sure. Go on.'

'Next came one from Mr Golf Pro saying that he is coming on board with us. The header showed that fax was sent to all the partners as well.'

'Of course it was,' Romy groaned, feeling herself sinking deeper and deeper into the quicksand that surrounded Sebastian Fox.

'Aah. Alan must have found out who Sebastian's new law firm is. A few rude words in this one. I might keep a photocopy for the Christmas party.' Gloria looked up at Romy, a big grin spread across her pixie face. 'But this latest from Mr Golf Pro is something else again, for your eyes only. And it reads like...a recipe for the perfect woman.'

'Give me that!' Romy spat out.

Gloria kept a tight hold of the sheet of paper.

'What does it say?' Romy asked.

'It says:

Dear Ms Bridgeport,

Further to our discussion I thought I would give you a running head start on our mission. In formulating the plans for my renovation, please keep in mind that I must in the end be capable of drawing an individual with the following non-negotiable criteria:

Easy on the eye

Able to string a sentence together
Must at least reach my chin when not in heels (old back injury means I cannot bend my neck for prolonged periods of time)
Employed
Hope that gives you somewhere to start.
Cheers, Sebastian.'

Well. He'd said he was willing and able with a bevy of ideas and it looked as though this could be the first. How helpful. What had she got herself into?

Gloria slumped into the guest chair, her eyes brimming with tears of laughter. 'Is he for real?'

'I'm afraid I really could not tell you.'

'If you had to make a list outlining the perfect man, what would it be?'

'Are *you* for real?'

Gloria pursed her lips and Romy knew it was either answer or be badgered for…forever.

'If I *had* to reduce someone to a list, my perfect partner would be serious, committed, optimistic, thoughtful and kind. He would remember my parents' birthdays and give up his window seat in a plane.'

Gloria grimaced. 'Sounds more like the qualities of a good priest than a good husband. But unfortunately I can picture who you are describing without even thinking about it.'

So could Romy and for that she was infinitely thankful. 'At least it's a tad more specific than that rubbish. How about you?'

'Did you not hear me regale you concerning Mr Fox's glorious butt an hour ago? And now I see there is a devious mind to go with it. Your Mr Fox is someone I'd happily bump into in a dark alley.'

If only the girl was not the most astute assistant she had ever worked with…

'Don't get ideas, Gloria. He's not *my* Mr Fox.'

'But now he's our client?'

'Looks that way.'

'Fantastic.'

Romy expected Gloria, who refused to wear skirts or high heels, claiming they were a form of bondage imposed by men to put women at a disadvantage, of all people to be outright offended by Sebastian's ridiculous list. But alas, she seemed to have quickly succumbed to the man's more flagrant charms.

Gloria leapt from her chair and practically skipped to the door. 'I'd be happy to take dictation for every one of your meetings with that one.'

Romy held her arms out, palms upwards in submission. 'If it will make your day.'

'Romy, that would make my year.'

Sebastian sat back in a dark leather chair in the office he kept in a cottage in the back yard of his Hawthorn home. He'd been in there all afternoon, catching up on correspondence, including forwarding the paperwork necessary to clear up his change of legal representation.

Now moonlight from the large bay windows streamed into the small room, spilling across glass cases filled with his sporting trophies, medals and pennants. Having them on display, even in this private room had been Melinda's choice. Sebastian would have put them in storage but Melinda insisted he keep them as a reminder of his wonderful successes.

All they did was remind him that he no longer professionally played the game he loved. A back injury sustained long ago had cut short his promising career before he had even hit his stride.

But he still preferred that cosy room to all others. His big house was too big. Too quiet.

Too lonely. It had been built to house a large family and as such had never realised its potential.

Rather than submit to the usual claustrophobia creeping up on him, to gain a much-needed boost of human contact, he dialled his sister's phone number.

'Hey, Melinda.'

'Hi, Seb. What's up?'

Sebastian heard the clank of cooking pans and pictured Melinda in the kitchen with the phone tucked between her chin and her shoulder.

'Just calling to say *hi*.'

'Hi.' She paused. 'What is it? Come on, it's dinner time. Hurry up.'

Sebastian had rung to let her in on his project. She wanted him to get a project and he had obeyed. But how on earth would he tell her his project involved the *babe* moulding him for marriage? If he was in the same room he just knew that Melinda would scuff him about the ears and accuse him of making a play for the woman. Which he most certainly wasn't. The thing was, he needed Romy. He needed her passion, her energy, her faith in a happily ever after.

Though Melinda would do anything for him, she could not do this. She just would not understand. She had gone straight from home into Tom's arms and had lived ten solid years with her wonderful family.

'Put Chris on.'

'He's doing his homework.'

'Come on. Put my nephew on or I'll call you Mindy forever and ever.'

'Fine. Chris!' she shouted out so that even the neighbours would hear. 'Uncle Seb's on the phone!'

Sebastian heard the muffled noise of footsteps thundering down the carpeted stairs.

'Here he is.'

'Thanks, Mindy.'

'You little—'

'Hey, Uncle Seb! Mum said you're taking us out Sunday. Where are you taking us?'

'I was thinking the zoo.'

'Yeah? Cool!'

Sebastian felt all his cares slip far, far away as he slumped back into his soft chair and listened to the excited babble of his young nephew.

CHAPTER FOUR

AROUND eight o'clock that night Romy and Gloria tumbled into Fables on Flinders in a mass of coats and scarves. The bar, with its wood panelling, burgundy leather seating and lawyerly clientele, may as well have been a law firm with a liquor licence.

Romy ordered a glass of white wine. 'You need more colour in your life, Gloria,' she said as Gloria sipped on her Black Russian through a straw.

They soon spotted Alan with a few of his cronies. He waved them over. They were like clones of every other man in the place, the men Romy associated with on a daily basis. They were young and successful in their tailored suits and handmade shoes but, considering their profession, these attributes were tempered by male-pattern baldness and premature pessimism.

'We hear you have stolen Alan's meal ticket,' one of the guys said.

'Jealous?' Gloria asked.

The guy shrugged and said nothing and received a good ribbing from the others.

'I am sorry, Alan,' Romy said. 'He didn't get any encouragement from me.'

'Don't worry, Romy,' Alan said. 'I've had a day to get over it. And I'm sure I will be able to put food on the table this winter. So is he giving you any trouble?'

She shrugged. 'Nah.' But that was the worst part. Since his *recipe* fax she had jumped every time her intercom had beeped or her phone had rung. She had expected him to come back, or send another fax or at least call. And since he had not, her nerves were shot.

'He's a big pussycat,' Gloria said.

'It's the big cats that you have to watch,' Alan said. 'They're smooth, they're quick and they're lethal.'

'Thank you, Alan. I'll be sure to remember that.'

Beside her, Gloria drew in a sharp breath and Romy saw her eyes widen. Romy followed their direction to find her very own tomcat standing by the table, with a Cheshire grin spread across his face.

'Evening, Alan,' Sebastian said. 'Hi, boys.'

The men all gave him hearty handshakes. Even after having dumped their firm he was still obviously a very popular bloke. A man's man.

His attention turned to Romy and her stomach flipped. With his hair slicked back, face freshly shaven, wearing an immaculate charcoal-grey suit with a matching overcoat he was a knock-out. She could sense Gloria all but batting her mascara-loaded lashes beside her.

Who was she kidding? He was a woman's man if he was anything. Though decked out in similar garb to those around him, Romy recognised that he was like a lion amongst the surrounding pack of hyenas. Ideas and plans bubbled excitedly to the surface just looking at him. Plans about their plans, of course.

'Were you looking for me, Sebastian?' she asked, struggling to keep her voice steady.

'That I was. Thought tonight was as good a night as any to get started on our project.'

Romy flinched. Her gaze swung around the table and she found several pairs of desperately eager eyes turned her way. If they knew that she, Romy Bridgeport, hard-nosed divorce lawyer, thought she could help Sebastian Fox, renowned playboy, land himself a wife for life there would be no living it down. But of course if she kept such a high-profile, lucrative client happy by succeeding in the task, then she would be lauded as the most innovative and hands-on divorce lawyer in town. Even partnership material?

So before any incriminating questions could be asked, she slithered out of the seat. 'Of course. No time like the present.'

Gloria plonked down her drink and made to follow. Romy all but shoved her back into her place as she shot her a warning glance. 'Stay, Gloria. Have one for me.' *And keep your mouth shut!*

She grabbed a hold of Sebastian by the elbow and all but dragged him from the table. Her friends waved their goodbyes amidst some barely hidden jokes and catcalls.

'What was that all about?'

'You just happened to be the topic of conversation before you arrived. They warned me you could be trouble.'

'What with?' He paused and then it seemed to dawn on him. 'With you?'

Romy's face burned in an instant, one of the pitfalls of having such pale skin. 'I hardly think that is what they meant.'

He appraised her face as he led her out the front door. 'They had cause to think as much. But you know what? You must be the first attractive woman for whom I have not had one thought of marrying.'

'Lucky me.' She had no idea whether to feel relieved or offended. She shot him a look as she slipped by and searched his face for any sign of the same intense reaction her body suffered in his presence. He smiled blandly back and she decided it was a one-way street.

Well, that was all the better. Physical attraction was a fickle thing. It came and it went and so long as one of them was completely unaffected it would slip away, unspoken. And nobody would be left a blithering, humiliated mess, which was the best one could hope for in a situation like that.

'But since you are already engaged I guess that lets us both off the hook,' Sebastian said.

She glared at him. 'Meaning?'

'Meaning you won't be looking to me as some sort of available suitor to take you away from all your worries.'

'And what worries would those be?' she asked between clenched teeth.

'You tell me.'

'The only worry that comes directly to mind is the fact that my time has been annexed by one client who I believe will be wasting said time. Anything you could do to sort that out for me would be much appreciated.'

'Alas, that's the one thing I cannot do.'

He grinned, her chest tightened and she could have slapped him for it.

'But at least we can focus on our project knowing we are both safe from each other's clutches.'

She tried to convince herself that the idea of being in his clutches could not have been less appealing. 'Well, that's just excellent. I always feel so much more comfortable with a new client once I am sure they feel safe from my clutches.'

'So, where do we begin?' he asked.

'Hmm?'

'With the project. Turning me into husband material for the next lucky Mrs Fox.'

She sensed the smile in his voice and hated that he knew he had her muddled. She was a ruthless lawyer, a thorough lawyer, and a lawyer who should be more clear-headed than her client. She looked up and found they were alongside Federation Square.

'Here?' Sebastian asked. 'Great idea. I've never been in here before.' Sebastian grabbed Romy by the hand, sending delicious, warm, unwelcome shivers up her arm, and jogged her up the steps and across the paving that led into the inner-city cultural complex.

Hundreds of people were seated along the paved expanse, rugged up in a rainbow display of picnic blankets and sleeping bags, pockets of air showing white from their warm breath, their bright eyes lit blue from a massive outdoor movie screen.

'Was this what you had in mind?' Sebastian asked. He leant in near to her, his voice tickling against her ear. 'I hardly see how I can meet the woman of my dreams here unless you plan to distract one so that I can sneak in under the sleeping bag with her.'

Romy shivered. In the rush to leave she had forgotten her coat back at the bar and felt distinctly cold in nothing but a sleeveless black dress, stockings and stilettos. Compared with the couples snuggled together beneath the stars she felt frozen solid.

'I wouldn't mind joining you there,' she said and as soon as the words had left her mouth she regretted them. 'I meant…'

A slow, easy smile lit Sebastian's face. 'Don't panic. I know what you meant.' He lifted a finger and ran it down Romy's freezing nose. 'So pink. I think frostbite is not so far away.'

Romy wrapped her arms tight around herself, her nose tingled from that one small touch and she stared up into Sebastian's captivating eyes, which reflected threads of silver from the big screen. Why one man deserved to be so charismatic as well as so inordinately handsome was beyond her. Somebody up there liked him. Everybody down here certainly seemed to.

Everyone except her, of course. She was attracted to him, but so long as she didn't like him, that hardly mattered.

'Come on,' Sebastian laughed, 'let's get you indoors.'

He opened his big, warm coat and wrapped Romy beneath it with him. Too cold to complain, Romy was content to snuggle against his warmth as they strolled along the edge of the multitude of rugs to the restaurant at the end of the complex.

Romy's skin zinged as the thaw fast melted away within Sebastian's solid embrace. She shuddered.

'Still cold?' he asked, his voice a low mumble against the back of her neck.

She nodded though it could not have been further from the truth. Taking her at her word, Sebastian slipped his right hand beneath the coat to rest it against her folded arms, the fingers inadvertently playing against the sensitive hairs on her arms. She wondered in alarm if his hands would burn from the touch, as her body felt aflame.

No matter his earlier assurance, she felt very much ensconced in the man's clutches. And instead of feeling trapped, it felt warm, it felt safe and it felt all too good.

As such Romy was beyond thrilled when they made it to the restaurant and she could extricate herself from his persuasive arms.

Although only a Wednesday night, the restaurant was packed.

'Hungry?' Sebastian asked, whipping his coat off and wrapping it around Romy. The coat swamped her. She was tall but he had not noticed how slender until feeling her against him. And now she was a good metre away, her arms defensively wrapped in front of her, he wished he were back beneath the coat with her.

'Starving. But no point. We won't get a table,' Romy said frostily, her eyes darting from his to the exit.

Even in the warmth of the restaurant Romy shivered, and he wondered if her recent trembling had been from the cold at all. It seemed their brief encounter beneath the coat had been a good deal more intimate than he had intended. That spoke of future trouble so he decided it was best to ignore it.

'Oh, I wouldn't know about that,' Sebastian said, motioning to garner the attention of the *maître d'*.

After a brief excited whisper to the cashier, the *maître d'* rushed past the three other couples in line to greet them.

'Mr Fox,' the gentleman gushed, 'welcome to the Dome. We are thrilled you have chosen to eat with us tonight. Your table is waiting this way.'

Sebastian held an arm in front of Romy to lead the way, but she held her ground. She glanced up at him, her nose still pink, her teeth still chattering, and her eyes delightfully confused. 'I thought you had never been here.'

'Haven't.'

'But you have reservations?'

'Nope.'

She glanced at the *maître d'*, who waited patiently for them to follow. 'He's giving you a table because you are…who you are?'

'Mm-hmm.'

'Because you used to hit a small ball into a slightly larger hole for a living you get to eat before these people who have been waiting longer than we have?'

Sebastian blinked. Then he glanced down the line of happy, chattering couples who were shuffling from one foot to the other, anxiously awaiting the moment they could take their weight off those feet.

Romy shook her head 'no'.

Sebastian took a deep breath and approached the *maître d'*. He pressed a hefty tip into the man's hand and said, 'Thanks mate, but please let these people through first. We'll just pop to the bar instead.'

The *maître d'* nodded with a slight but definitely impressed smile then turned his attention to the couple at the front of the line, who had no idea what had gone on. They just continued to chatter amongst themselves as they followed the leader through the restaurant to a great table in a sheltered corner of the room.

His dates usually basked in the extra attention his infamy provided. This was the first time he had been put in his place over it. And he liked it. See, he was learning from her already.

'Come on.' Sebastian put his hand in the small of Romy's back and led her to the public bar, where they found a small table in amongst the hordes. He tried to tell himself that he was being polite but he knew better. He was striving to retain the pleasant prickles of awareness her recent contact had generated.

They reached a table in the bar. Romy kept his coat wrapped about her. When she sat down she knocked over the vial of salt and without missing a beat she grabbed a pinch and threw it over her shoulder before settling down more comfortably in her chair.

The waiter was at their table in a flash. Romy ordered a glass of white wine, he ordered a straight Scotch and a plate of potato wedges. Romy caught the waiter by the arm and with a big smile begged for extra sour cream. The waiter blushed at her attention.

'Not exactly what I had in mind,' Sebastian apologised, once the waiter had left.

Romy shrugged. 'I'm so hungry I could eat a *raw* potato.'

'They serve that back in the restaurant I hear.'

Romy's smile reached her eyes before she suppressed it. 'Yet I was willing to give that up in the spirit of fair play.'

'Fair play? That, coming from a divorce lawyer?'

'Sure. Or maybe you would prefer in the spirit of the rules of the game?'

'You always live by the rules?'

'If at all possible. Without rules there is chaos. And I am not a big one for chaos.'

'So you were put on this earth to bring order to the world.'

She sat up straight, cocked her head on the side and her eyes lit from within. 'Sure. Why not?'

Sebastian was amazed afresh at her luminosity. Pick the right subject and despite herself she was so animated. So dazzling. So full of energy. No matter how hard she tried to suppress her vivacity beneath a stern and serious veneer, it shone from her. And if he had any chance of being able to rekindle his passion, his old desire to devour life, he was very glad Romy would play a key part in his transformation.

'And why were you put here, do you think?' she asked.

Why was I put here? Sebastian asked himself. The answer should be easy. He had a great many passions in life. Sports? His family? None of it seemed quite as consequential as bringing order to chaos.

Before he could answer her, the waiter came promptly back with their drinks and wedges. The young man saved Romy's extra sour cream for last. He offered it to her with such delicacy it might as well have been resting on a velvet cushion.

'Thank you so much.' Romy grinned at the young man and he turned to putty. So he wasn't the only one mesmerised by her radiance.

'So what's the verdict?' Romy asked before biting off the tip of a sour-cream-lathered wedge. Her eyes were such a clean neat blue, like the sky on a crisp autumn day. And when she smiled those magic eyes popped, making the colour so vivid it was head-turning. No wonder the waiter was dumbfounded.

'I am here on earth…to buy you a sumptuous dinner you will never forget.'

Out of the corner of his eye he saw the waiter still hovering. It was time for the pretty boy to move on. Sebastian paid him then shooed him away with a tilt of his head.

* * *

'I have some questions,' Romy said, feeling it was time to bring the night back to a professional footing.

'I'm thirty, six feet two and my favourite colour is…' Sebastian reached out and snuck a hold of a strand of her hair. 'What do they call this?'

She tucked her hair behind her ear, breathing out slowly as it slipped from his fingers. 'I meant about our project.'

'Ooh.' He feigned sudden understanding. 'OK, shoot.'

'Why go through fiancées, and now wives, the way you do? Why not just date? Why go through the rigmarole of engagements and marriage?'

His smile faltered but only for a moment. And when it returned it was different. Could it have been serious? 'Because, Romy, I want children, a wife, the works.'

It had been a question to throw him off course and instead it seemed to have knocked him exactly on course and left *her* floundering. She felt herself balancing on the edge of something new. There was a sudden and unexpected fragility about the conversation as though if she forced it too hard the bubble would break. This felt different. This felt real. And she was awash on an unfamiliar shore without her note cards to back her up. She nibbled at her little fingernail.

Children, a wife, the works, she thought. For someone whose work revolved around the consequence of language, the order of his listed desires grabbed her right off the bat.

'I could refer you to a colleague of mine, from another firm, whose speciality is adoption.'

He seemed to consider his words. 'That is very kind of you. But I am quite determined to have a family of my own.'

'That's fair. Except you seem to have brought a long line of unsuspecting women into the equation.'

'Not unsuspecting.'

'Excuse me?'

'None of them have been in the dark as to my agenda.'

'OK, then. Perhaps you have gone about it in the wrong order. I believe love, marriage and *then* the baby carriage is the time-honoured order of things.'

His eyes narrowed and he stared at her. Although she felt as if they had taken a small step forward, she had not known him nearly long enough to read a look like this. It was a dark look. Clouded. She held her breath and her pulse slowed while she waited.

'Excuse my hesitation,' he finally said. 'I had to take a moment to believe I had heard the word "love" coming out of a divorce lawyer's mouth in place of terms such as *mutual financial benefit*.'

She did not think that was what his pause had been about but she would follow his lead...for now.

'Of course marriage should be about love. It should be solid, upstanding and worthy.'

The clouds in his eyes cleared and that magnetic spark of humour returned and with it her racing pulse. Her chin raised a fraction.

'You disagree, I take it,' she said. 'You probably think love is a term created by greetings-card companies to sell valentine cards.'

Sebastian leaned forward, with his elbows on the table and his chin on his knuckles. He raised his eyebrows and that mischievous grin spread across his face and Romy knew the barb had bounced right off.

'Oh, I don't know about that. It was just the *solid, upstanding and worthy* part that silenced me. I rather think of love as an unexpected, accelerated inferno. It should grab you by the throat and not let up for a moment as it whirls you on its relentless, ravishing ride.'

Coming from him, it seemed all too possible. And all too alluring. She swallowed hard.

'Next question,' he said, thankfully giving her a way out.

She had a million. But there was one other she simply could not hold back.

'You left the meeting early yesterday because you had a date.' OK, maybe not so professional, but she was itching to know.

A small smile played at the corner of Sebastian's mouth. 'I didn't hear a question in there.'

'I told you before, I don't want to be wasting my time if you already have some floozy on the back burner.'

Less and less professional, but how could she even hope to be professional with potato wedges on her plate and footy replays blaring from the bar behind her?

'Trust me, there is no floozy.'

Romy worked her bottom lip between her teeth. 'Fine, then. No floozy. A girlfriend? An intended? Who did you have to meet?'

'There is no fish. No floozy. No girlfriend. No fiancée. Just me and the big, wide future out there. And every Tuesday at three there is a standing appointment with my nephew and his little league touch-football team.'

Romy was stunned into silence. Almost. 'You had a date with your nephew?'

'His name is Chris,' Sebastian said. 'He's my sister Melinda's eldest.'

He reached into his back pocket and pulled out his wallet. Romy glanced over the photograph of three gorgeous kids rolling about in the arms of their adoring uncle.

'He's ten. Then there's Thomas, Junior. He's a terror. And lastly we have Delilah. She's four and precocious and reminds me a great deal of you.'

Sebastian leant back in his chair and watched her with a smile so filled with affection it slammed her against the back of her seat. *Professional, Romy, professional.*

'I can assure you, Sebastian, it has been a long time since I've worn pink overalls and nothing else.'

He looked her over as though he thought that was a mistake. 'It's not her fashion sense. She's bright and diverting and knows exactly what she wants. Oh, and of course there's the Barbie connection. That was the clincher.'

She stared him down but knew he was being serious. These kids meant the world to him and when it came to them there would be no falsehood. She knew without a doubt he would be a great father. And maybe, just maybe she could play a part in giving him that chance. She would have to cling to that if she was going to succeed.

'Next, I want to talk to you about your list.' Lawyer Romy was at long last back in charge. 'How would you say Janet and your previous fiancées and girlfriends and…whatnot stood up against your rigorous criteria? Would it be safe to say they all fitted the criteria perfectly?'

Sebastian continued to smile but she saw the moment the glimmer left his eyes. 'I see your point. Not specific enough, was it? OK, let's start over.'

The glimmer was back. Sebastian grabbed a napkin off the table and a pen from his jacket pocket. 'Top to bottom. Hair colour to size of feet. Now you still didn't tell me what they call your hair colour—'

'Sebastian, I don't have the time or the inclination to help you if you are not going to take it seriously.'

He laid the pen on the napkin, looked her directly in the eye, and Romy held her breath.

'Romy, you do have the time because I am paying you for your time. As for the inclination, I just know that you see me as a project you simply can't refuse. I can see it in your eyes. You are dying to give me a makeover.'

Truth be told, Romy knew she would not change a hair on his perfect body. But she also knew in her heart of hearts that there *was* something about him that she could help. Beneath the jokes and the charm there was a downtrodden spirit? A sadness? A hopelessness bred from not being able to get it right? Since she was brimming with antidotes for all of these possibilities, she knew she had to help him.

'If this is really going to happen I think we need to clear some things up. I am not going to get you dates, Sebastian. That, I am sure, you can handle on your own.'

By the number of women in the bar who had not been able to tear their eyes away from him since he walked in, she thought it should be a cinch to find someone who was attracted to him, and out of the hundreds of those women finding someone compatible should be easy.

'If I am going to help you it will be by getting you to the stage where *you* can determine when the right woman for you comes along. Not just a woman with whom you can spend your free time, but the woman you are meant to spend your life with. If we are to do this, I will be deadly serious and expect you to be the same. So are we doing this for real or not, Sebastian? Tell me now.'

She half hoped he would laugh and say to forget it. But her other half was getting used to these strange little chats, was looking forward to the peculiar little jolts she felt in her stomach when he turned one of his megawatt smiles in her direction. It was as if she was getting all the buzz of the beginnings of a new relationship without any of the messiness inherent in such a leap. It had been a very long time since she had experienced such feelings and she knew that it could very well be her last.

She waited, her anxiety level reaching screaming point. No, she wanted him to say he was for real. She knew now if he laughed it off she would be devastated.

'We're on,' he finally said.

She let out a breath of relief. 'Fine. Give me that pen.'

She grabbed the pen and napkin and drew up a couple of columns. 'You are obviously a list man, so let's go with that. We will start with parameters for the assignment. You have given me the positives, of a sort; now I want you to tell me about everything that went wrong, starting with girlfriend number one, and we will sort out the source of your previous relationship failures so this time it won't happen again.'

Sebastian raised an eyebrow at her. 'Who says they were my failures? Maybe they were their failures and I just got caught in the crossfire.'

'You have been engaged three times, married once, and they're the ones my researchers knew about! No. There's a pattern here and I am determined to figure it out.'

Sebastian bit his lip. The last thing he wanted was to go into detail about his relationships. He had steered clear of therapy, he had avoided marriage counselling, he had even managed to evade hearing the whys and wherefores from the exes themselves. And he had no intention of going through the wringer now.

He reached out a hand and covered hers, staying the pen she had been resting so eagerly over the napkin. 'Let's not, OK?'

She stared at their entwined hands as though entranced. A few heady moments later, she swung her eyes to stare at him. And for the first time since he had set eyes on her, her guard came crashing down. And her gaze spoke volumes. He felt the current buzzing between them too, and while he soaked it up to experience she looked like a deer caught in a pair of headlights. Her mouth fell open, her eyes grew wide and her chest rose and fell in deep breaths.

And, though it was expressly against the rules he had set out for himself in coming to her in the first place, he took the pen from her hand, laid it gently on the table and wrapped her hand in both of his, revelling in its tender warmth. Her hands were so pale and soft he could make out the veins running her hot blood beneath the skin. Utilitarian fingernails cut almost too short with no polish. So refreshing compared with Janet, whose nails would better be described as talons; long, hard, blood-red and costing hundreds of dollars in upkeep.

Her hands were so soft. Little time in the sun, no time doing labour any harder than typing on a computer keyboard. He had a sudden urge to take her trembling hand, pull it to his lips and kiss the soft inner warmth of her palm. He ran his fingers over her knuckles and saw that, also unlike his exes, no rings adorned them. No rings. And most significantly—

No engagement ring!

CHAPTER FIVE

'SEBASTIAN FOX, right?'

Romy snapped out of her trance and slid her hand from Sebastian's warm grip. She flicked a glance in the direction of the voice and saw a group of young male executives staring at Sebastian.

One suited man dragged mesmerised eyes from her dinner partner and looked her over. She knew in a heartbeat he was comparing her to that bevy of beauties Sebastian had been photographed with during the course of his public life. She had the duelling urges to throw off Sebastian's huge coat, grab a compact and fix her lipstick, and to scream out, *I am his lawyer, not some bimbo, you jerk!*

She turned back to Sebastian, fuming, expecting him to feel very pleased with himself at the attention. But her temper subsided when she saw that, though he was smiling as he nodded to the young men, the smile did not reach his eyes.

'See,' one young man said as he slapped his friend on the arm, 'I told you it was him.'

'What can I do for you boys?' Sebastian asked, his voice cool.

'We saw you at the Coolum Classic, oh, six or seven years ago. We were there on holiday and our dads took us to watch you play. My dad reckoned you could have been the best Australia had seen if you had not had that accident.'

The flinch behind Sebastian's eyes was slight, but it was there. Accident? It rang a bell but Romy did not remember reading of any accident in the dossier. Must have been some golfing mishap. Or perhaps he'd put out his back performing some tantric feat with a perfect set of blondes. If so, it served him right.

'Oh, I wouldn't know about that, guys, though do tell your father thanks.'

'Shall do.' The guys stood by and kept grinning, as if they were just waiting to be invited to join the table.

'Is there something else I can do for you?' he asked and Romy was amazed he could remain so easy and polite in the face of such an invasion of privacy, especially when she just knew they had hit a deeply hidden nerve.

'Nope. Great to meet you, that's all.'

The young men each took turns to shake his hand, all the while looking at him as if he was some sort of god. Romy even earned a handshake from the one who had seemed to think her a tad below his hero's regard. When finally they left, Sebastian reached for a potato wedge and ate it in silence.

'Does that happen often?' Romy asked.

'Often enough.' And in the way he spoke she knew it was not as easy for him as he made out. For a guy she once thought revelled in living in a media spotlight, she now thought it was more likely patience and good humour that got him through rather than abundant ego.

'Always young guys?'

'Not always guys.' And then he grinned.

Damn him! Every time she felt herself being drawn to him, and to his cause, he would pull out the tomcat card. *No. Not damn him*, Romy thought as she fell deeper into his beautiful smile. *Thank heaven!*

The more he reminded her of his bad-boy reputation, the better for her and her diminishing wariness. Romy wished she could still detest him, though with every moment in his company she was finding it harder and harder to do so.

But rather than get caught in the mesmerising minefield of grey-green eyes she brought the conversation back to where it should never have left in the first place.

'If we are not going to analyse the mistakes you have made in the past, how about highlighting the good points? Concentrate on what went right.'

'I quite enjoyed the bedroom arrangements.'

She just stared at him.

'I love having someone else to hit the snooze button for me.'

'Well, then I'll add that to your list of prerequisites, shall I?'

Sebastian picked up the pen and placed it in Romy's hand. 'Excellent. You go ahead and do that. And while you're at it, I'm allergic to dishwashing so she'll have to be willing to take on that job.'

'You're allergic to dishwashing liquid?'

'No, just dishwashing.'

'So acquire a dishwasher.'

Sebastian pointed to Romy's napkin with its empty columns. 'I thought that was what we were doing here.'

'OK, that's it.' She put down the pen and stood. 'It's late and I'm not on the clock. I'm going home.'

'Fair enough. Where's your car?' Sebastian asked, standing and pushing in his chair. 'I'll walk you.'

Her shoulders slumped in the huge coat. 'It's Wednesday. Wine night at Fables. I took a cab.'

'Just in case you had a blinder?'

She shot him a withering look. 'Hardly. I just don't drink and drive. Not even on one glass of wine. Not only for legal and safety reasons, it's bad karma.'

Sebastian paused.

'Bad karma? Salt over the shoulder? And I'm sure I saw a family of elephants with raised trunks taking up valuable shelf space in your office. From this morning's voluble comments regarding the sanctity of marriage, I would have thought you would be a great believer in destiny. But I seem to see a pattern that demonstrates quite the opposite.'

She shook her head. 'I've seen enough people rely on destiny and get it very wrong to let it control my life.'

'So you don't plan to let yourself close your eyes, fall into destiny's hand and see where she takes you?'

Romy allowed herself to imagine doing just that; relinquishing the strict control she had over her head and her heart and allowing chance to guide her where she would. Sebastian made it sound so easy, so liberating. But no. Romy had quashed that option long ago. She knew exactly how that scenario would end.

She shrugged. 'I don't like surprises.'

She waited for Sebastian to say more but he seemed satisfied. For now. He reached out and settled the coat more squarely on her shoulders before buttoning it up for her. 'Come on. I'll grab you a cab.'

He led her through the bustling bar, a protective hand on her lower back. Did the guy have a furnace in his fingertips? Even through the heavy wool, Romy could feel his natural heat.

Once outside even Sebastian's magic fingertips were not enough to keep her warm. The air was heavy with coming frost. Sebastian whistled up a cab that pulled to a screaming halt at their feet. Of course. Everyone else served at the pleasure of Mr Fox; why should late-night cabbies not do the same?

Romy undid the buttons of Sebastian's coat and handed it back to him.

'Keep it for now. I'll get it another day.'

She shook her head, 'no'. The scent of his soft soap had drugged her enough for one night;

she did not need it invading her home. 'I'll pick mine up at Fables before I head home.'

His eyes narrowed for a moment, and Romy had the feeling she had been found out, that her awareness of him was written across her face. But he nodded and took back the coat, wrapping it around him. He opened the door for her and called out Fables' address to the driver.

Romy hopped in the car and fastened her seat belt, eager to just get going. 'Goodbye, Sebastian.'

'See you soon.'

Romy shot him a brief smile then tugged the door closed. She was grateful when the driver took off straight away.

First thing Thursday Romy made her way to the firm meeting with her usual drink made to order by the lovely Hank and a made-up mind. Sebastian Fox had to go.

She had barely slept the night before. Her dreams had starred none other than his truly, and all of them were unrepeatable in polite company. And that had been the last straw.

When she was with him, the thought of making a success of his project was so tempting. Only when alone, without him sitting across the table scrambling her thoughts, was she able to think things through more clearly. Only then did lawyer Romy have free reign rather than being the befuddled, unhinged, wound-up Romy she was around him.

The problem was, it wasn't the infuriating-playboy Sebastian that was keeping her up at night, it was the glimpses of the kind and attentive, shy and private man. And she knew no matter what a fabulous professional and personal coup the successful conclusion to his project would be, it was not worth the mess the guy was making of her inner peace.

As such she had every intention of giving him up. It was the only way her future plans would succeed without a hitch, which was just how she liked her plans to go.

By now the whole firm would know of Sebastian Fox's arrival and she would need to get in quick if she was to explain why she did not see him as a client fit for their firm. Romy took her second-row seat, back from the partners' table, and was ready when, after the initial good-mornings and pats on the back, hers was the first name called.

'Ms Bridgeport. It seems we have you to thank for bringing to us some new business,'

Gerard Archer, the senior partner, called out, his voice cutting into her thoughts like the voice of God.

'Yes, sir,' she said.

But before she could draw breath to begin her thoroughly researched spiel Gerard's voice boomed, 'Speak of the devil.'

The whole room turned to face the door and Romy felt the cool fingers of dread clasp themselves around her throat, thus cutting off all speech. She turned slowly and found the man in her thoughts leaning casually in the doorway, looking good enough to eat in a debonair three-piece suit and traditional striped tie.

She stifled a groan as Gerard bellowed, 'I would like to introduce you all to our new client, Sebastian Fox, who has kindly agreed to pop his head in this morning.'

Sebastian smiled graciously, and Romy saw that many of the tough-as-nails litigators were looking up to him as if he was some sort of hero. If Romy wasn't so flabbergasted she would have rolled her eyes. Instead she turned and faced the room at large, but found the eyes burning into the back of her head almost as daunting as if she were staring them down.

'For those of you who don't know,' Gerard continued, 'Mr Fox has transferred all of his personal legal needs into our hands, including management of his substantial stock portfolio and numerous real-estate interests. I am sure he won't mind my saying what a huge boost it will be for us not only in the funds that will swing our way but also in industry exposure.'

She just knew Sebastian would be smiling and nodding with his usual easy grace.

'However did you manage this feat, Ms Bridgeport?' Gerard asked and Romy wished she could dive into her cup of tea. But alas, since she had only ordered a small…

'I beat him in a lawsuit, sir.'

The partners around the table erupted into laughter.

'Well, I'm very glad you have come on board, Sebastian,' Gerard said. 'It takes a secure man to put a positive spin on a negative situation. You will fit in beautifully with our firm's philosophies.'

'Glad to be here, Gerard.'

A small amount of happy applause rounded the table and the door shut with a soft click and Romy knew Sebastian was gone. She was infinitely thankful. If she'd had to spend the next half an hour with him at her back she did not think she would have made it.

Gerard turned to face Romy again. 'Excellent work, Ms Bridgeport. Just the sort of client-focused work we want to see in our young guns. It will be up to you to keep him on a short leash. So all of your other cases will be reassigned whilst Sebastian has your full attention on this mystery project of his.'

Romy seethed in her seat.

Gerard swept a pointed finger around the table, encompassing everyone in the room. 'It's the clients that make a firm grow, not the cases. Those who bring them in will reap the rewards. Well done.'

Romy nodded her thanks as she fought to keep her lips buttoned tight and her thoughts on the meeting at hand. It seemed Sebastian was hers to keep before she even had the chance to let him go. She was now under instruction to help him to the ends of the earth. A smile lit her face. This could be more fun than she'd anticipated. She was after all a girl who took her job very seriously.

'How did the meeting go?' Gloria asked when Romy stormed into her office. 'Well, by the looks of it.'

'I want Sebastian in my office ASAP.'

'Who wouldn't?'

'Gloria…'

'I'm just saying you have to admire a woman who knows what she wants and isn't afraid to admit it!'

'Gloria, that's not what I meant and you know it…'

'Sure, boss. I'll convince him to hot-tail it over here, shall I?'

'He's in the building.'

Gloria's eyebrows rose. 'I knew you gave your clients the most focused attention of anybody here but I think having him tailed is a little excessive.'

'He came to the morning meeting.'

'Oh. Well, then. Whatever Romy says Gloria does. Will you want the door closed when he arrives? Do not disturb and all that?'

'Gloria…'

'I'm on it! Sheesh! Can't a girl have a little fun?'

A little fun, Romy thought as she swung back into her chair. That's exactly what every girl deserved. Romy picked up the phone and called in favours left, right and centre.

It was not long before Sebastian rocked up and Gloria led him into the office. Romy thanked her assistant and had to take another look. Gloria had swathed her lips in pink gloss and had even styled her hair into a more feminine arrangement than its usual carefully orchestrated spiky shambles. Romy raised her eyebrows at her assistant, who even managed to conjure an entirely feminine blush. Romy was at a loss for words.

Gloria led Sebastian to his seat. 'Mr Fox, would you like a coffee? Tea?'

Romy waited on bated breath for Gloria to say 'Me?', which thankfully she did not. She felt Sebastian's pause and wondered if he was waiting for the same proposition. The twinkle in his eyes would suggest as much.

'I'm fine. Thanks anyway, Gloria.'

'We have infusions. Ginger? Chamomile? Peppermint?'

Sebastian held up a hand to stop her. 'Less and less my cup of tea.'

Gloria laughed. Or more like tittered.

Romy finally found her voice. 'Yes, thanks ever so much, Gloria. We'll be right from here. Just let me know when our other guest arrives.'

Gloria nodded. 'And who might that be?'

ALAMEDA FREE LIBRARY

'You'll know it when you see him.'

Gloria left, but not without poking her tongue out at her boss from behind Sebastian's back.

Now they were alone, his polite smile morphed into something entirely different. 'Gloria made it seem urgent. She said you *wanted me* in your office ASAP.'

Romy clenched her hands beneath her desk, picturing Gloria's neck in between them. 'I figured you would be available.'

'And here I am. All yours,' he said. He leant back and put his arms behind his head, looking all too sure of himself.

She reached for a file from the cabinet at her side, happy to hide her wry smile behind a curtain of hair. *Smile away, Sebastian. You have no idea what you're in for!*

'I thought since you were in the building,' *and are becoming chummy with the senior partner over my head,* 'we can get our plans underway at once.'

'You've made plans?' he asked. 'For us?' His voice was low and Romy thought a little husky. But she chose to ignore that.

'Hmm. You're not the only one with a *bevy of ideas*,' she said, thinking back to his list. Well, if he wanted to play games… 'According to the partners, you are now my number-one client, I am to cease all other cases and your concerns should be my number-one concern.'

'Really?'

She heard the smile in his voice and wasn't at all surprised. But she had her reasons for making him feel relaxed. 'Really. So, I have organised some help.'

'Some help?' She looked up and saw his smile waver ever so slightly and she just could not wait to show him what her sort of help entailed.

'Yes. To show you how *seriously* I am taking our project, I have organised an assistant to aid us in our quest to make you into a new man.'

'Justin is here,' Gloria's dismayed voice buzzed over the intercom.

'Send him in.' Romy felt her nerve endings sing with anticipation.

'So who's this Justin?' Sebastian asked. But before Romy had time to explain, in flounced Justin in top-to-toe, figure-hugging crystal-blue leather, red plastic sandals and a blonde Afro bouncing atop his head and no explanation was needed.

'Romy! Darling! Long time no smooch!'

Romy stood and walked over to her guest, her eyes flicking to Sebastian, who stood as well. Despite his evident shock, politeness had long since been bred into him.

She gave her friend a big kiss-kiss. 'Justin. So lovely to see you again.' Romy felt Justin pull out of her embrace, as he must have seen the object of his…help.

'Is this my guy?' he asked, his voice an exaggerated whisper. 'If it's lady's choice, he is!'

'Sebastian Fox,' Sebastian offered, shaking the man's hand without a moment's hesitation. His smile seemed genuine and the shock most people felt at seeing Justin for the first time was missing from his excellent poker face.

'Justin. Pleased to meet you.'

'Justin…?' He turned to Romy, looking for a surname.

'Just Justin,' she explained, standing back, watching the strange interplay between the two men, one exceedingly polite, the other flamboyant as all get-out.

'Has been for years, sweetheart. There comes a time you become so infamous you don't need a surname any more. Our Romy could be there.' He reached over and plucked at the neckline of her black crossover jersey top, his distaste at the classic look obvious. 'If only she'd let me dress her more. Red, darling! Wear more red.'

'You're not here for me today, my friend.'

Justin turned back to face Sebastian front on. He took a couple of steps closer to Sebastian and his gaze roved over every spare inch, and for the first time her exclusive client looked scared. Romy could barely contain her delight.

'That's right,' Justin enthused. 'I'm here all for you, my handsome little bundle of man flesh.' Then he reached out and gave Sebastian a thumping slap on the behind before springing back and clasping a hand to his mouth. 'How could I resist?'

Romy bit her lips together to keep from laughing out loud. She shrugged and shook her head, simply unable to answer his perfectly reasonable question. She'd had to overcome the urge herself on several occasions.

She took a deep breath and swallowed her laughter. 'Now down to business. Sebastian, you may have figured that Justin here is an image consultant.'

Sebastian obviously had figured no such thing but he finally managed to string together a sentence. 'You think I need an image consultant?'

'Honey,' Justin took over, 'the world at large sees you as a has-been sports pro with too much money to know what to do with it and both eyes on the ladies. If anybody in this room needs an image consultant…' He fluffed a hand around and let everyone complete the sentence for themselves.

Sebastian looked at Justin as though he had sprouted an extra head. 'Do they really?'

Justin shrugged.

But Romy saw the shock in Sebastian's face and it cut her to the quick. Justin was not one to hold any punches, and Sebastian really seemed disconcerted by his brusque revelation.

Could he really not know that was his public image? she thought. Then it dawned on her.

He knows. And he's afraid that it's true. That's what she had felt at the Dome. That was the sadness, the downtrodden spirit. Sebastian had begun to believe his own bad Press.

Well, no wonder he'd come looking for her.

CHAPTER SIX

'I THINK JUSTIN is exaggerating to prove a point,' Romy said, shooting Justin a look to quieten him. 'Though you must see that you are a media target. Since you have been a success in so many arenas, they love to cut you down in those in which you have not been so… successful.'

'My relationships.'

'Exactly. And, since most women you meet will have heard of your reputation, that is your first hurdle to finding someone willing to take you on. We have to show the world at large that above all things you are a nice guy.'

'You think I'm a nice guy?'

Romy sensed that his question was genuine and she faltered. The answer was yes. She really wished that she could wipe the misdirected unease from his face by telling him as much. But to admit that to him would only send them down a very different track, and that was the last thing she wanted.

Romy looked to Justin for help but he shrugged. 'Well, that's what we're here to establish.'

Sebastian glanced at Justin again and she could see the wheels turning.

'Don't worry, Sebastian. Justin is not into creating clones of his own bizarre image. He's a pro. He's the best. He will help you.'

'OK. If this is what you want.'

Her heart continued to reach for him. She ached to tell him what she really thought. How much his innate kindness had hooked her, even more than his charm and good looks ever could.

'This is not about what I want. It's about what you need.'

Romy's intercom buzzed. 'Romy, Libby Gold is here to see you.'

'Haven't they assigned her another lawyer?' Romy asked, feeling downhearted at the thought.

'Apparently but she demanded to see you and nobody else.'

That raised a smile. The partners could hardly argue with that. Romy glanced at Sebastian who was watching her carefully, and Justin, who was watching Sebastian carefully. 'OK, let her know I'll be out in a minute.'

She grimaced at the two men in her office. 'Seems I will have to leave you two boys all alone for a moment. Use my office. Chat. Get to know each other. And I'll be back as soon as I can.'

Justin gave her a quick air kiss then pulled out a huge tape measure from his pocket. 'All righty, then, let's get you measured up. Do you dress left or right?'

Romy gave Sebastian a big wink then closed the door on the two men. Gloria was at her desk looking busy. Too busy. She finally stopped typing and turned on Romy.

'Why are you subjecting him to Justin?'

Romy shrugged, the picture of all innocence. 'He's the best.'

'He's a freak!'

'Gloria…'

'Sorry. You're right. There's nobody like Justin. If anybody can make him over into Mr Nice Guy it's Justin. Though why anyone would want to change one inch of that man's gorgeous—'

'Gloria, where is Libby Gold?'

'In the library.'

'Thank you. I'll be back in a bit. And don't you disturb them unless you hear screaming. From either party. Promise?'

Gloria slumped in her seat and examined her fingernails. 'I promise.'

Romy rushed to find Libby sitting in the library. She'd had her hair done, she wore make-up and she was obviously wearing new clothes.

'Libby! You look fantastic!' Romy gave her a big hug.

'Do you really think so?'

'You bet.'

'I was...I was hoping that Jeffrey would think so too but I thought I should check with you first.'

Romy swallowed hard as they both sat on a big soft couch. 'You did this for Jeffrey?'

'Of course. If he is going to take me back, I am going to have to make it worth his while.'

Romy leant forward and took Libby's shaking hand in hers. 'Has Jeffrey made any overtures of the kind? Has he asked to move back in?'

'Well, yes.'

Romy's heart threatened to break. She had seen it so many times in so many incarnations, and it never, ever worked out well. It was up to her to make sure Libby knew that she would be better off moving on.

'But it's the papers, you see,' Libby bumbled on, her face turning a blotchy pink as she told her story. 'He had been seeing…the lady in question but it never went further than a couple of dinners. Nothing happened. And now he wants me back.'

The newspapers. The tabloid Press. She knew someone else whose life had been lived in such a forum. And she was beginning to realise how they could tell the true story with enough of an inaccurate flavour to get it so very wrong.

'Romy. I'm really so unsure. You tell me. What should I do?'

'Libby. Take him to dinner.' Romy could not believe the words coming out of her mouth. She, who was infamous amongst the legal fraternity for never losing a client back to their spouse, was about to advise a client to give it another go. But once she started the words tumbled out all too freely. 'Give him a chance to tell you his side of the story. Listen to every word. Listen with your head, and with your heart. And then whatever you decide to do I will stand by you one hundred per cent.'

Libby all but burst into tears as she leapt into Romy's arms. 'Oh, thank you so much. I was sure you would tell me I was doing the wrong thing but it felt so right. Wish me luck.'

And Romy, who did her dandiest to make sure luck played no part in her life, wished for it with all of her burgeoning heart. Libby gave her another hug before all but dancing out of the library.

Romy glanced at her watch. Fifteen minutes had gone by. She all but jogged back to her office, her footsteps gaining momentum, anxious more than she imagined she could be to know how the two men had got on. If her plan had panned out, Justin would be flirting with the guys at Reception and Sebastian would be long gone.

She felt a twinge at the thought that if Sebastian had run and their plan was done for, was that really the best outcome for him? Or for her?

She rounded the corner and her steps faltered.

Justin was leaning back in Gloria's chair, his feet on her desk. Sebastian was swinging Gloria round in a magnificent dip and was regaling the two of them a story that had Justin rocking back with laughter and Gloria barely able to keep on her feet she was giggling so hard.

Justin caught sight of Romy first. 'Romy, darling! You're back. And not a moment too soon.'

Sebastian stood up, bringing Gloria with him. Gloria straightened her clothes and, blushing madly, rushed behind her desk, shooing Justin out of the way.

Sebastian put his hands casually in his trouser pockets and leant back on the desk, his eyes not leaving Romy for a second and his mouth expanding into a knee-melting smile.

Romy turned her attention to the relative safety of Justin. 'So you had a productive time, I take it. You mapped out a plan on how to reconstruct his image.'

'Forget about it,' Justin insisted. 'He's a gem. Leave him be.' He spun to face Sebastian, his face alight with inspiration. 'Though I would add more leather to the wardrobe, OK?'

Sebastian gave Justin a thumbs-up and a wink, which sent him into hysterics once more.

'Leather?' Romy said, in astonishment. 'More leather will improve his reputation? More leather will throw him into the path of his perfect partner?'

'Put that behind into leather and his reputation will be irrelevant.' Justin held up a hand, which Sebastian neatly slapped with a high five. 'Got to go, my lovelies. Gloria, the lip gloss is a revelation. Romy, more red, please. And

Sebastian, don't you go changin'. Mm-mmm. I hope to see you again soon.'

'Count on it, my friend.'

Justin waved a hand to cool an imagined hot flush, then he was gone, his gravity-defying hair seeming to give off its own source of light until he rounded the corner, leaving the three regular people staring after him.

Romy turned on her heel and marched into her office.

'Well, that went well,' Sebastian said, following and lying back in her sofa.

'Glad to hear it.' Though she wasn't at all. Justin was meant to scare him off. Send him running, screaming, never to darken her doorway and steal away all of her spare time again.

'So what's next? An agent? A manager? A pimp?'

Romy ran a frustrated hand through her hair. 'No. That's what you've hired me for.'

'*Touché*. Just promise me, whatever you have in store for me next, no more blue leather trousers.'

'Fine. No more blue leather, I promise. So next is…' She looked at her watch. She had booked a long lunch with some people she used in her work from time to time. But, since Justin had not done his job of sending Sebastian running from the building in terror, she would have to put them to use as *next*.

Romy hastily wrote a note for Gloria, and practically threw it at her through the doorway.

'Next I have some more experts I think can help.'

'Who are *these* experts?' Sebastian asked, the grim smile on his face showing he knew just what she was thinking.

'A psychologist, a marriage counsellor and a pastor—'

'Walked into a bar?'

She glared at him, wishing and hoping her panel would all be wearing blue leather.

'A psychologist, a marriage counsellor and a pastor will be waiting in the conference room. For you. To spill your secrets.'

At the word 'secrets' she saw a flicker of misgiving flash across his eyes but it was gone in a heartbeat. She remained silent, all but daring him to refuse. But this was what he had hired her for.

Sebastian stood up, rubbing his hands together. 'Well let's go, then. Into the lion's den.'

'Fine.'

Romy led the way downstairs, slowing the pace to give her lunch guests the time to switch to expert mode.

Then Romy left them to it. She thought Sebastian might open up and get more from the session if she was not there. So she returned to her office and did casework on Libby Gold's file. But after an hour of Olympic-level fidgeting she summoned up a hasty tray of coffee and biscuits and made her way to the conference room.

She opened the door carefully and stopped, slack-jawed, to find the most unbelievable tableau being played out before her.

Sebastian was standing behind the pastor, they were holding on to a broom like a golf club and Sebastian was obviously helping him perfect his swing. The psychologist was crawling around on his hands and knees looking for a rolled-up bit of paper they were using as a ball and the marriage counsellor was pretending to be a flag waving in the breeze above the hole on a putting green.

'Found it!' the psychologist called out. He pegged the makeshift golf ball to Sebastian, who caught it easily in his left hand before plopping it before his student.

'Well, I assume your work here is done,' Romy said through clenched teeth. All four looked up at her like kids with their hands caught in the cookie jar.

'Not quite,' Sebastian quipped. 'I haven't yet fixed Jessica's slice.'

Romy looked to the marriage counsellor holding on to the *flag* and shook her head. At least the woman had the good grace to blush as she mouthed 'sorry'.

'OK, playtime is over. And I am very disappointed in the lot of you. I am seriously questioning your loyalty to me right now. Off you go.'

The three 'experts' brushed themselves off, the pastor helping himself to a biscuit on his way out. 'See you Sunday, Romy?'

'Yeah, we'll see about that,' Romy quipped before planting a kiss on the old man's cheek.

Once they had gone, Romy laid the tray on a lamp table by the door and stood with her hands on her hips.

'So what's next?' Sebastian asked, his voice teasing.

'Dinner,' she said with a flourish, a brilliant plan fast forming in her mind. If she really wanted to reform him, to show him what it would take to make a successful marriage, she knew just where to take him.

'Dinner?' Sebastian repeated, a winning smile kicking at the corner of his mouth. He eased his lanky frame against the edge of the conference table, his eyes bright at the suggestion.

She nodded. Then watched in amazement as his eyes darkened at her agreement. 'A business dinner, of course, so the location is my choice.'

'Another of your experts?'

Romy nodded.

He bowed. 'As the lady wishes.'

As he rose he looked her dead in the eye. Something clicked inside her, her focus shifted, and she saw it. The same latent attraction she felt for him. And she knew it had been there since day one, but from behind her mask of self-protection she had chosen not to see it.

'Did you have to do that?' she asked, her voice low.

'What?'

'Hijack my intervention like that?'

'It wasn't my fault. Before I knew it they'd pounced on me for advice and when I tried to refuse they threatened to give me a bad report card. Sorry.'

He was not a bit sorry and she knew it. She clenched her palms at her sides, glad she had no fingernails or she would have drawn blood.

He was bad and she had been so good for so long. He didn't follow the rules and she never stepped outside of them. He got her so riled. So hot under the collar. But she knew there was a fine line between heated anger and burning passion. And at that moment that line was drawn on the carpet at her feet.

She could feel the lick of awareness arching between them. There was no denying it. He remained leaning against the table, his discerning gaze watching her, unblinking. He smiled and she stared. That mouth. That sensual, sexy mouth.

It was against the ground rules she had set for herself and followed for so long. Too long. When it had been hers alone she'd had a chance, but when she felt the same desire reflected in his eyes it was inescapable. And she would not be the one to stop it. She leant on the door behind her and it closed with a soft, meaningful click.

Romy stepped over the imaginary line at her feet as she sauntered over to grab the broom handle, which was resting against the conference table. She ran her hands along its vertical length until its tip rested comfortably on the ground. She shuffled until her high-heel-shod feet were shoulder-width apart, her short, tight skirt hiking a few centimetres higher up her thighs. She lined up the scrap of paper towards the plastic cup on the ground and swung. And missed by a mile.

Sebastian casually walked around the table, picked up the scrap and continued around the table, until he came to a stop directly behind her.

'May I?' he asked, gesturing to the makeshift golf club.

'It's your dollar,' she answered, her voice a husky whisper.

Sebastian moved until he was flush up against Romy's back. He dropped the makeshift ball in front of her club. His soft trousers brushed up against her naked legs, goosebumps standing to attention at the pseudo-innocent caress. Warmth radiated from his length and swept in pulsing waves over her exposed skin.

His arms slowly crept around her torso until his bare forearms and hands covered hers and she was in his clutches once again. She was wrapped so snug she could feel the pulse beating down the length of his arms, and its speed and intensity were almost a match for her own.

'Here,' he whispered against her hair, the curls wafting to tickle her ear, sending delightful shivers down her neck. 'Your hands need to be a little lower. Just relax your arms.'

Was he kidding? It would take an elephant tranquilliser to make any part of her highly strung body relax.

'Like this?' She smoothed her hands down the length a little lower and found herself bending slightly to accommodate.

'Perfect.' His voice had dropped an octave and the deep, delicious sound reverberated along her spine. 'Now, take a deep breath.'

She did as she was told.

'Eye the hole.'

Their heads turned as one to the paper cup.

'Eyes back to the ball, swing back and swing forward, following through, with your eye never leaving the ball until that magic sound, plop; the perfect symbiosis of golf ball and hole. They are deeply attracted and want to be together. The vast green distance between them seems too far, too hard. They just need that extra push to send them to where they are meant to be.'

Romy swung and hit. The raggedy paper ball sped and tumbled towards the cup before hitting a piece of carpet fluff and veering off at the last second.

Romy could feel Sebastian's laughter as he shook behind her. 'Sounded good in theory.'

She turned to face him. 'I believed you.'

Their faces were mere inches apart and Sebastian had still not unwrapped himself from around her. All of the sensations of warm skin against cool, cloth-covered limbs against nude left her as everything focused on her hard-beating heart and the temptation of those smooth, ready lips before her.

Romy felt her body rotate. Sebastian was turning her in his arms so that bit by bit she revolved to face him.

A short, sharp voice in her head told her to pull away but it was squashed beneath a steady rise of another voice telling her that she should go for it. Cool, controlled Romy had been in charge for all too long and would be in charge again any minute. It was only fair to give impulsive Romy the chance to stretch her wings.

The door to the outer office bounced on its hinges and both Romy's and Sebastian's head snapped to face the noise. The door sprung open and a man appeared silhouetted on the threshold.

'Darling!' the man called out. 'I'm back.'

CHAPTER SEVEN

'ANTONY!'

Romy tore herself from Sebastian's grasp. He had the contrary urge to drag her back and finish what she had started but a semblance of self-control took over and he put his disobedient hands in his pockets.

He watched her like a hawk as she jogged over to the doorway and the man picked her up and swung her about as though she were as light as a kitten. When the man placed her lightly back to the floor he bent and placed a familiar kiss just to the side of her soft lips; those enticing lips that had been Sebastian's for the taking only seconds before.

It felt so inappropriately as though his heart was being ripped from his chest by a set of rapacious feminine claws. He ached to turn away but there was no point; unless he put his fingers in his ears he could not stop from hearing the entire conversation.

'When did you get in?' Romy asked.

'Just now,' the man answered in a strong Bostonian accent. 'I tried to call last night but you must have been screening your calls and you know how I hate answering machines. So, fill me in. What have you been up to?'

Sebastian fought the urge to tell the guy she'd been at dinner with him, wrapped in his coat.

'Working, mostly,' Romy said before he had the chance.

'And just now?'

Sebastian gritted his teeth.

Romy hesitated. 'I am with a client.'

'Nice work if you can get it,' Antony said, miming a golf putt.

'Ah, Sebastian,' she called out.

Time to put on the show of his life. He plastered a smile on his face and walked over to the couple, taking the time to discern the gentleman at Romy's side. Tall, slim, decked out in casual attire that reeked money. Expensive watch. Designer sunglasses perched atop his head. Manicured hand resting proprietarily on Romy's hip.

'Antony,' Romy began, her voice all but quivering, 'this is Sebastian Fox.'

Antony held out his spare hand. 'Antony Lucas. Pleased to meet you.'

'Any friend of Romy's…' Sebastian tendered, shaking the man's cool hand.

Antony laughed and Sebastian was not entirely sure it was sincere. 'I'd like to think I'm a good deal more than just that.'

How much more? Sebastian longed to ask. *Just tell me you're the elusive fiancé and be done with it.* But alas, no such final declaration was forthcoming.

Antony's eyes narrowed and again it hit Sebastian that it was an affectation. 'Have we met?'

'Wouldn't think so.' Sebastian folded his arms and stood with feet shoulder-width apart. 'What do you do?'

'Lawyer,' he said with a shrug suggesting it was obvious. 'I work for Archer's big-brother firm. Primarily in the Boston office and I am a guest lecturer at Harvard Law.'

Well, bully for you, Sebastian thought. 'I haven't been to Boston in years. Maybe I just have one of those faces.'

'How about you, Sebastian? How do you fill your days?'

Sebastian mimicked Antony's shrug. 'Mostly I watch daytime TV.' He risked a quick glance at Romy and found her head bowed and a smile spread across her face. If that wasn't enough to buck a man's hopes he had no idea what was.

Antony's mouth dropped open but then his eyes narrowed and this time Sebastian knew it was for real. Antony nodded and smiled. 'I only wish I had that sort of time.'

'Antony!' Gerard, the senior partner, called from outside the doorway before waltzing in and giving him a great bear hug. 'The driver found you OK?'

'Sure did. Thanks for that, Gerard. Glad to be here.'

So Antony left word with the boss he was coming but not Romy? Sebastian thought. *What a guy.*

'Now, tomorrow the partners and senior staff are flying up to Sanctuary Cove in Queensland for a couple of days of golf. I've saved you a spot,' Gerard continued.

Antony shook his head. 'Wish I could. But I'm here on business, not pleasure.'

Sebastian glanced to Romy, whose mouth instantly turned down at the edges. But, supertrooper that she was, she bucked up in an instant.

'Besides, I'm not much of an outdoor type. Give me a chess board and I'll gladly take you on.' Antony spun on his heels and clicked his fingers at Sebastian. 'Fox, right? The golf pro?'

Sebastian nodded.

'Knew I knew you. Saw you win the Boston Open several years ago. Hole in one on the seventh. You were a hotshot.'

Sebastian could barely raise a smile. This guy was just too smooth. Too slick. Too damn close to Romy, who hadn't looked him in the eye since the guy arrived.

'This is too perfect,' Antony said to Sebastian. 'Why don't you take my place at Sanctuary Cove? Give yourself a weekend off from Oprah?'

Gerard all but burst a seam. 'You're more than welcome, Sebastian. We'd be honoured to have you go a round with us.'

Sebastian was about to politely ease himself out of the kind offer when Antony all but pushed Romy into Sebastian's arms and said, 'And take Romy. She's a great little golfer.'

'But you only just got in,' Romy whispered.

'I'll be busy all day tomorrow anyway. Go. Have fun. Stick close to this big guy here and maybe he can teach you a thing or two.'

Sebastian rocked from Antony's chummy slap to the back and had to restrain himself from returning the favour with fervour. 'As long as Romy's willing, I'm on board.'

'Of course, you'll both come,' Gerard blustered. 'The plane's at seven tomorrow morning. Get the details from my assistant. How long you here for, Antony?'

'A few days at most.'

'Drinks one night?'

'Of course.'

Gerard left, and Romy, Sebastian and Antony were again alone.

Why he felt so much animosity for the guy he did not wish to analyse. Antony's appearance at that moment had probably saved him from blowing it entirely with Romy. If they had given in to their growing fascination with one another it could very well have spelled the end of everything he had come to her for in the first place. He should have felt relieved, rejoicing that Antony was a real guy. But he had not felt less like rejoicing in a long time.

Sebastian unfolded his arms and sank his hands deep in his pockets. 'I'll be off, then, Romy. I think we were just about finished here.'

'OK.'

'Antony.' Sebastian shot the man a brief nod, simply unable to shake his hand again, then he strode from the room.

After a few moments he heard the click-clack of Romy's heels as she jogged after him. It took for her to take a hold of the sleeve of his shirt before he could make himself stop. He did not feel like giving her an inch.

'Yes?' he asked, avoiding looking her in the eye. He knew just what her expression would be. Apology. Contrition. Embarrassment.

'Sebastian, look at me.'

She asked. He looked. That was all it took.

And there was no apology. No contrition. No embarrassment. Just confusion and barely restrained desire and a desperate need for him to still like her. She ducked her head, unable to meet his gaze any longer. The tables had certainly turned. But he knew exactly how she felt and he could not make her suffer for it.

He hooked a finger beneath her dainty chin and lifted her head. 'What can I do for you, Romy?' His voice sounded very far away.

'I just wanted to make sure everything was OK.'

'Sure. Today was very…informative.' Today he wondered if he really was the selfish man she had once denounced him to be. He wondered if he was a dog in a manger, only wanting what he knew he couldn't have.

But a part of him hidden deep below all of these concerns wondered if maybe now she was out of reach he realised what he had in front of him. What was very possibly slipping through his fingers.

'And tonight?' she asked.

'You still wish to take me to dinner?'

'I did say it was a business dinner, part of my plan.'

'That you did. And Antony?'

She glanced over her shoulder at the empty hallway beyond. 'He's…busy tonight.' She swallowed. She wanted to say more. Much more. He could see it in her huge, expressive eyes.

'Fine. I'll meet you back here after work.'

Finally she nodded. 'OK.'

Sebastian slowly drew his finger away. He gave her one last little tap on the tip of her sweet nose then turned and left before he would have to follow his instincts, which, despite all that had just happened to wrench her from him in so many ways, was to follow the tap with a kiss.

Romy trudged back to her office. Gloria met her there with a plateful of fridge-cooled Tim-Tams. And Romy knew her assistant, the most well-informed person in the building, knew exactly what had gone on downstairs.

'Antony found you with Sebastian, didn't he?'

Romy took a Tim-Tam and bit down hard on the smooth chocolate biscuit. Then it dawned on her. She turned on Gloria, her voice rigid. 'You sent Antony down to me, didn't you?'

'Of course I did.'

'Knowing we were—' Romy slammed her mouth shut.

Of course she did! Of course Antony had came to Romy's office to see her as soon as he arrived and of course Gloria would have pointed the way. And why wouldn't she? It was entirely Romy's fault she had almost been sprung in what would have been a most compromising position, not Gloria's.

Though she still had a funny feeling that Gloria had known exactly what she was doing.

'Did you know Antony was coming to town?' Gloria asked, her voice soft.

Romy shook her head. 'Not today. But I knew he would be back.'

'Of course he's back. You asked him to give you a month to think about it and it's been a month.' Gloria began bouncing up and down on the chair. 'So?'

'So?'

'So what are you going to tell him? What's your answer? Are you going to marry him, or not?'

And that was the question of the day. Though at that moment the answer was anybody's guess.

Sebastian dived into the swimming pool, the chill water sapping the heat from his body. He took long, hard, raking strokes, exhausting himself, forcing his mind to concentrate on lactic acid pumping through his veins rather than on her. After fifteen minutes he came up for air to find Tom lying on a deckchair, wrapped to the neck in a polar blanket.

'Hey, buddy,' Tom said. 'What are you doing?'

'Felt like a swim,' Sebastian said between heaving breaths.

'So I see. You do realise it is the middle of winter?' Tom asked, his teeth chattering.

'So? Once you warm up it's OK. Come on in.'

'Ain't going to happen, buddy.'

'Sore knee still?' Sebastian asked, finally able to raise a smile.

'Sure. That'll do.'

Tom waited. And Sebastian knew it was explain or suffer the consequences. 'It was all true. She bloody well has a fiancé. And an American at that!'

'By *she* I assume you mean the lawyer.'

'Of course I do. I mean, she never denied it but she never admitted as much either.'

She still hadn't, exactly. But that Antony guy had been something. If not a fiancé then he was a boyfriend, or a lover, or something equally atrocious.

'But I was beginning to think it was as you said, a ruse to keep slathering, newly single males, who must follow her around everywhere, at bay.'

Of whom I am turning out to be one, Sebastian thought, filthy at himself. *Pathetic!*

'But no?'

'But no.' Sebastian pushed off from the edge and swam several punishing laps of the pool. When he pulled up Tom was still there.

'So what if she didn't have a fiancé?' Tom asked. 'Would that have made a difference?'

'What do you mean?'

'Would you have asked her out on a *date*? Would you have considered her girlfriend material…and the rest?'

Sebastian wished he had not brought the subject up. The fact was she did have a fiancé, or something, which should have been the perfect scenario, so the last thing he needed to admit to himself were answers to those sorts of questions.

'She's my lawyer, Tom,' he said as though that would answer the loaded question.

Tom bundled the blanket around himself and stood to leave. 'So. I married my dentist's receptionist. What difference does that make?'

Sebastian continued to tread water.

'Are you staying for tea?'

'Nope. I'm going out to a business dinner with Romy.'

Tom raised his eyebrows but said nothing.

'Go inside, Tom. I won't be long.'

Tom waved a finger from beneath his rug and shuffled inside. Sebastian went back to his gruelling swim, desperate for the freezing water to drown out the disturbing images of Romy in another man's arms.

It was after seven when Sebastian sauntered up to Romy's office. Gloria was gone but Romy's office light was still on, so he leant in the open door and gave the wall a light knock.

When she looked up at him her face was unreadable. But tired. So very tired. He'd had a not nice afternoon and had been hoping she'd had much the same. And now he knew she had, he took it all back.

'By dinner,' he said, 'I sure hope you meant you, me, a secluded little grotto, candlelight, oysters and way too much wine.'

She watched him from under lowered lashes and he saw a new level of mistrust. Maybe that was for the best. Maybe that was what they needed again to get back to the old dynamic where she hated him and he thrived on it. And he would have left it at that, determined to control his hormones, if she had only not swallowed hard and said in the sweetest of most drawn-out whispers:

'Just don't. OK?'

Whoa. He held up his hands in submission, a playful grin carefully masking the pile of very serious thoughts tumbling about in his mind. 'You can't blame a boy for trying.'

Romy nodded in agreement and tried a self-deprecating smile on for size. It felt slipshod but she hoped he would not notice.

Candlelight? Oysters? Alone with Sebastian? As soon as the words eased from his practised mouth, the image sprang fully formed into her mind, as though it had been at the ready, just waiting for her to call it up from the deepest recesses of her mind. She imagined Sebastian leaning over with an oyster in hand, ready to tip it into her waiting mouth…

She shook off the image, knowing he was watching her. She whipped on her coat, and grabbed her handbag off the back of her door handle. At the door she turned back and said as brightly as she could, 'Now, if you'd had Dean Martin playing on the stereo you might have been on to something.'

'Nice wheels,' Sebastian cooed as Romy walked him to her new midnight-blue Jaguar. 'Looks as if I picked the right girl…to look after my interests.'

If he had blinked he would have missed the unsure glance he received. She was still on edge despite her attempts to keep it light.

'So where are you taking me, Ms Bridgeport? Somewhere unique, I hope.'

'I guarantee you have never been there.'

'Excellent.' He rubbed his hands together. 'I'm all in for new experiences.'

'Considering your run of betrotheds, I don't doubt that for a second.' He knew she was reminding herself more than him. Romy opened the passenger door. 'Keep your mind open and you might just learn something.'

Sebastian regarded Romy covertly as she slid into the driver's seat and methodically put on her seat belt, adjusted her mirror and fiddled with the air-conditioning vents before turning on the car. A fake rabbit's foot dangled from the key chain. And it was a sharp reminder that this was not a woman willing to take chances voluntarily.

'You don't mind me driving?' she asked, an uneasy half-smile lighting her beautiful face.

'Not at all. Makes the trip all that much more intriguing, knowing I am totally at your mercy.'

The smile faltered for a moment before she turned back to concentrate on the road. Yep. She was as tense as he. 'I'm afraid since you're the client I am the one at the mercy of your wallet. Any time you want to stop this, we can.'

Again that unsure glance. Sebastian's stomach curled in an unfamiliar tangle of knots. If she really wanted him to pull the plug, she was about to be disappointed. The truth was the only thing keeping him whole, keeping him sane, was her.

If only Romy would just bestow upon him the easy smile she gave Justin, or rib him with the easy manner she showed Gloria. Maybe that would be enough. If she just took him into her small circle of friends, maybe that would rid him of the ache that had settled in his stomach the moment another man had called her 'darling'.

But he knew it would not be enough. Where only days before all he had needed were her company, her vibrancy and her hope, now those ethereal qualities did not suffice.

What he wanted was her.

So what if Antony was her fiancé? He wasn't her husband. Until then she was fair game. And he had a feeling that, though it was rubbing painfully against her grain, she was feeling the same way.

'I don't want to stop, Romy. Take me where you wish and I will follow.'

So Romy took Sebastian to the heart of perfect married life. She took him to dinner with her parents.

CHAPTER EIGHT

ROMY was met at the door by a manic ball of golden fluff.

'Grisham!' she called out as the dog leapt straight into her waiting arms. She knelt and rolled him onto the ground, giving his fluffy belly a brutal rub.

Sebastian knelt at her side and rubbed behind the giddy dog's floppy ear. 'What on earth is it?'

'A Labra-doodle, we think.'

'You think? You haven't thought to ask him?'

'I don't speak dog.'

He sat back on his haunches and his hand leapt to his chest. 'Something Romy Bridgeport cannot do? I am shocked.'

She smiled back at him. 'He was a Christmas return. A lady we knew bought the kids a puppy for Christmas and the fun wore off once the feeding and cleaning became part of the bargain. When we heard, we decided to take him in.'

'"We" meaning your parents.'

'I live in an apartment. They have a huge back yard. I take him on holiday every month or so.'

'Holiday?'

'Sure. A day trip to the beach. A couple of days at my aunt's farm in Wallan. Chasing kangaroos is a favourite pastime, isn't it, Grish?'

No comment from Sebastian, though Romy could feel his gaze burning into her. For a guy with a big mouth she suddenly found his silence more daunting than his cheek.

'Romy! I thought I heard the door.'

Romy was glad to see her mother walking down the hall at that moment. She enveloped her in a warm hug and as usual felt as if she could stay in that embrace forever.

'Hey, Mum. You look great.'

Her mother raised a hand to her silver bob. 'Had a haircut. And this time they gave me an eyebrow wax.'

Romy stood back, admiring the handiwork. 'Looks great. Very nice job.'

Her mother's eyes left her and raked over the man wavering at her side. She glanced back at Romy and raised her shapely eyebrows. 'Is this who I think it is?'

Romy shook her head vehemently, a hasty blush heating her cheeks. Somehow she had managed to stay away from that loaded subject matter with Sebastian; the last thing she needed was for her mother to make a big deal of it.

'No, Mum. This is Sebastian. A client of mine. Hope you don't mind setting an extra plate for dinner.'

'Of course not.'

'Sebastian, this is my mother, Cynthia.'

Cynthia held out a hand, which Sebastian shook. 'Pleased to meet you, Sebastian.'

Sebastian gave Cynthia a gallant nod. 'Likewise, Cynthia. You have a charming home.'

'Thank you. Now, take off your coat and jacket. No need to be so formal. We do run a home here, not a manor.'

Romy stood back and watched as Sebastian shucked off his outer layers and handed them over to Cynthia.

'Shall we?' Sebastian cocked his elbow and Cynthia took a hold, but not before shooting her daughter an impressed look over her shoulder. Romy frowned and shooed her mother away.

After a quick stop off in the bathroom to wash dog slobber off his hands, Sebastian sat down at the dining table.

The banter flew fast and furious from one end of the table to the other with each family member attempting to outdo the last. George cut the roast and Cynthia served. George made derisive comments about bitter mint jelly and Cynthia complained his slices were too generous. And it was all accompanied by cheeky smiles. Romy subconsciously played with the end of one loose curl, a gentle smile played at her lips and her eyes never left her parents.

This was Romy at home. This was Romy with the people she loved. She was soft, serene and secure. And unlike the perfectionist who amazed him with her energy, or the gamine that tugged at his smile, or the vamp that tugged at a different part of him, this Romy played havoc with his insides. His stomach had grown progressively tighter as the evening evolved and he knew it was not from hunger.

'Extra potatoes?' Cynthia asked.

By Romy's soft blush Sebastian knew it was not the first time he had been asked. He blinked before shifting his gaze from Romy to her mother. 'Of course, Cynthia. Pile them on.'

'You should know you're the first client Romy has ever brought over for dinner, Sebastian. Is this some sort of parole thing? Do you have to eat a good home-cooked meal every day or go back to jail?'

'Mum, he's not a criminal. He's a business client.'

'I know that, sweetheart. Now you're spoiling my fun.'

Cynthia turned to Sebastian with a wink and he could not help but laugh. It gave him immediate insight into Romy's similar nature.

'What sort of business are you in, Sebastian?' George asked, finally joining the conversation.

'I am an investor, sir.'

'Hardly sounds like a business to me.'

'Dad…'

But her father did not waver. 'Investor in what? With what?'

Sebastian shot Romy a reassuring smile. 'I made some money playing professional sports. And when I gave it up I made some wise investments that left me…self-sufficient.'

George's face lit up as if a light bulb had gone off over his head. 'Knew I knew the face. Fox, right?'

Sebastian nodded as he took a spoonful of potato.

'You were pretty good. Bugger of an injury, that. Surprised you can still walk.'

Sebastian felt Romy's eyes on him.

'Romy and I were talking about you the other night!' Cynthia clapped her hands together. 'You're the stud!'

A stud, hey? He shot Romy an enquiring look but her mother's comments had been enough for her to look away.

'Romy, why didn't you tell me this was *him?* He looks shorter on television. Now I finally have some news to tell the girls at poker night.'

Romy raised her head. 'It was last-minute, Mum.'

Sebastian caught Romy's expression from the corner of his eye and he guessed its measure. The 'girls at poker' probably had all sorts of news of their grown children getting married, and having babies of their own. It was probably hard to throw 'my single daughter bought a new luxury car yesterday' into that sort of mix. Having someone infamous come to dine was right up there with the best of uncomplicated gossip.

And then he remembered Antony. He would be the perfect foil for her mother's interest, so why would her parents not have met him? Unless their relationship *was* a ruse, a rumour she had started to keep not only slobbering single men but also her parents off her back on the subject of a ticking biological clock.

Sebastian's heart picked up the pace. Was Romy engaged or wasn't she? Every time he had slipped it into the conversation she had neither refuted nor verified the fact. And even when he'd met Antony he had not introduced himself as such. Antony had said he would like to be considered more than just a friend. Well, what if he wasn't? If Sebastian had been in his shoes he would have told any man in the room how much Romy meant to him.

Sebastian watched as Romy stood to pour more water into everybody's glasses. Did her throat feel as dry as his?

He had once intimated that her fiancé, real or not, was the one keeping them from each other's clutches and he had a feeling that his jest had been spot-on. By the end of the night he was going to know about her fiancé one way or the other.

'Come on, Sebastian,' George chastised, 'eat up. Cyn's roast is usually dry at the best of times. If you leave it on your plate any longer, you'll be eating dust.'

Cynthia grizzled good-naturedly at her husband. Sebastian did as he was told and happily finished off his second helping of the very tender and absolutely delicious roast.

An hour later, Sebastian was seated in the den with George while Romy and her mother caught up in the kitchen. George drank herbal tea, but Sebastian refrained. No coffee in the house, George explained, as Cynthia was a tyrant when it came to his blood pressure.

'You still play?' George asked.

Sebastian knew he meant golf. They always did. 'Sure. How about you?'

'Since I retired I go twice a week if I can.' The elder man sipped at his drink, trying to hide his wince. 'Romy too if I can pull her away from work.'

Sebastian nodded. 'So I've heard. We are off to a golf trip tomorrow with the firm. Can you give me any pointers on her game?'

'Only that when she puts her mind to something she is not to be deterred.' George shook his head. 'Don't know where she gets it from.'

'She seems to regard you both very highly. So I'm sure you can both take credit for her fortitude.'

George shrugged. 'I wouldn't know about that. She's a girl of her own heart and mind and has been since she was a kid. Got a tattoo when she was sixteen, you know. We expressly forbade it but she did it anyway. And since that moment there's been no stopping her.'

A tattoo? Well, well. *A tattoo of what?* Sebastian wondered. *And, even more importantly, where?* 'Would you have wanted to stop her?'

George looked up and Sebastian saw there was a sharp mind beneath those soft, friendly eyes. 'Every now and then. You may have noticed she can be a bit stubborn.'

Sebastian smiled. 'That I have.'

'And there are times when you just have to keep trying to get through her thick skull. Lucky both her mother and I are of persistent natures so we have managed to keep her on the right path when she has threatened to veer.'

Sebastian nodded, happily soaking up every little ray of light into Romy's complex personality.

'Are you of a persistent nature, Sebastian?'

'Oh, it depends really. I can be, when its called for. But I think I am a man who also knows when he's beaten.'

George smiled. 'That's the thing about Romy. She never does.'

* * *

'He's just gorgeous,' Cynthia gushed as Romy helped her wash the dishes.

'That he is,' Romy agreed. Denying the obvious would only have perked her mother's interest even more.

'And he's single?'

'For the moment.'

Romy felt her mother's eyebrows fly heavenward. 'Meaning he is not one to stay single for long.'

She wondered and not for the first time why that was. She understood why it would have been easy for him to find women willing to be with him but she was not convinced that was reason enough for him to leap straight to engagement so often.

'So he's a single client who could not keep his eyes off you all night.'

'Mother—'

'I'm just saying, he's attractive, he's well off and he likes you. He's a catch.'

'Believe me, he's the type of catch you should throw back and quickly,' Romy said, 'before you get food poisoning and are sworn off fish for life!'

'OK. OK. You obviously know him better than I do.'

'I do.'

'But if I was any younger and your father was on one of his work trips—'

'You ladies need any help?' Sebastian asked, leaning casually in the kitchen doorway. Romy spun to face him and her face was blanched of colour, bar two bright pink blotches high on her cheekbones. He wished he had been there a few moments earlier to know what conversation topic had brought her to that point of mortification.

'I thought you were allergic to dishwashing,' she threw at him with such vehemence he had a good idea what the conversation topic had been.

'But not drying up,' he explained, taking up a spare tea towel which was hanging over the oven handle. He nudged Cynthia out of the way and she gratefully took a seat at the kitchen table.

'You always did bring home the charmers, Romy,' Cynthia said, her eyes flashing with enjoyment. 'Must be your father's influence.'

George chose that moment to wander into the room. He took up a seat next to his wife, leant back in the chair and undid the top button of his trousers, groaning in relief as the pressure about his waistline was eased.

'Please, no!' Romy buried her face in her rubber gloves. 'Sebastian really does not want to hear stories about me.'

'Sure I do,' he said.

'She was always a high achiever,' Cynthia continued on unabated. 'Wouldn't be a part of a team unless she was captain. And wouldn't date anyone on the team unless he was co-captain.'

'Aah,' George said, 'you mean Liam.'

'Now, *he* was a charmer. Lovely boy. Could drink George under the table. Shot for shot of Lambrusco at Christmas time. What a riot!'

Romy wore a strained smile.

'What happened to him again?' George asked.

'He lives in Paris, dear,' Cynthia said in a loud whisper. 'You know that. He dropped out of university in his third year.'

'Why was that, again?'

Sebastian could sense Romy's distress but he did not know how to protect her from her parents' unintentional damage without embarrassing all of them.

'Because he followed a dancer who won a spot dancing at the Moulin Rouge,' Romy finally spilled.

'The Jennings girl,' her mother finished helpfully. 'Pity. He *was* a charmer. You ever dated a dancer, Sebastian?'

Sebastian flinched as the conversation suddenly swung back his way. 'Not yet.'

'Good. Capricious things, they are. Not to be trusted. How about a lawyer?'

'Mother!'

'Fine, fine. So what was your mother like? From what I have heard, you're a veteran in the affairs of the heart. Do you succumb to all that Freudian mumbo-jumbo that boys go for girls like their mothers?'

Sebastian picked up a dish and dried it extra-slow. 'I wouldn't know, Cynthia. My parents both died in a light-plane crash when my sister was a baby and I was just two years old.'

He felt Romy's attention zero in on him like a heat-seeking missile. But he had to get her parents' stifling interest away from her love life and if this was the way to do it…

'Oh, Sebastian,' Cynthia said. 'I'm so sorry. Were you adopted?'

'Not exactly. I was shuffled between foster parents and orphanages for the first several years of my life.' Sebastian paused for a moment, to swallow down the bitter memories of extreme loneliness that threatened to close off his throat.

He realised his hands were empty because Romy had stopped washing. She just stood there, staring at him with a wet dinner plate dripping in her hands. He finally had to reach over and take it from her hands and that was his big mistake. As he took a hold of the plate, his eyes skittered to clash with hers. She was watching him with such unbridled interest, her big eyes calculating and weighing up every snippet of information to add to her HELP SEBASTIAN dossier.

But it was more than that. Her eyes held not sadness, or guilt or sympathy, which he always feared he would have to deal with when talking about his past, but dawning understanding. And then he knew he was not opening up to Romy's kind parents, but to Romy, who had only tried to get him to this level of trust in order to help him.

He shot Romy a smile, to let her know that it was all OK, amazed that he was the one having to lend support at this time rather than the other way around. Then on he went.

'And then when I was near ten, I was lucky enough to be taken in by the Gibsons, a foster family with a house by the beach, near Byron Bay. So from that time on I grew up in a household that held between—' he stared at the ceiling, trying to remember '—eight and probably twenty kids at a time.'

'Phew!' Cynthia uttered.

'Phew, indeed. It was like nothing I had ever known. I went from years where I had nobody to never having a moment alone. My foster father was sports mad. We had interfamily sports carnivals every weekend. It was like living in a big summer camp, by the beach, hanging out with your friends at school and at home.'

'Wasn't your sister with you?' Romy asked.

He shook his head. 'Since she was a baby at the time...she was adopted straight away by a very nice couple. We found each other again when I was about twenty. She was eighteen and married with her first baby on the way. Now she has been with Tom for ten years and they have the three most amazing kids you could ever hope to meet.'

The room was hushed with an unearthly quiet. The dishes had stopped clanking, George's chair no longer scraped and even Sebastian's racing heart had slowed to a normal pace. That had been a heck of a lot easier than he'd thought it would be. He wondered why he hadn't simply swallowed his pride and told Romy from day one.

He looked over at her and she was still watching him, but now it was from beneath lowered lashes. So whatever was running through that mercurial mind of hers was hidden.

'Dishes are clean, Mother,' Romy interjected, finding it beyond difficult to draw her attention from Sebastian. But she had to; she knew he'd done more than his fair share of sharing. When she had done none. 'Time I take our beleaguered guest home.'

'Fine, fine. Off you go.' Cynthia helped George to his feet, and together they saw Romy and Sebastian to the door.

As Romy walked Sebastian to the car, he had his hand at her back. He was so polite. It was bred into him. And now she knew by whom. A lovely couple who fostered dozens of children and managed to create this ambitious, successful and wonderful man.

This man who had grown up as a lonely little boy only to finally find solace in numbers. This man who since leaving this loving home had run from the arms of one woman to another, desperate to recapture that same intense feeling of family. This man who set her nerve endings on fire with the softest of touches. Who had her aching for his kisses with the smallest curve of his smile. And earlier that day had had her ready to throw away all she had struggled so hard to build just so she could have one long, hot moment in his expert arms.

When they reached the car Sebastian leant in to take the keys. Romy leapt away from him as though burnt but he seemed not to notice. He unlocked the door, held it open for her and waited until she was belted in before handing over the keys.

Romy leant over and unlocked the passenger door, her mind so full she had no idea where to start. Sebastian slid into the passenger seat and they took off. In silence. Perhaps Sebastian was at as much of a loss for what to say as she was.

Halfway along the Monash Freeway Sebastian perked up and said, 'If you have another expert lined up as after-dinner entertainment I am throwing in the towel right now.'

Romy laughed so hard she had to pull over to the slow lane. 'I wouldn't blame you. My folks are…interested people. Retirees, you know. Their life is pretty much the six o'clock news and poker gossip. I should have known the life and times of a sporting hero would be too much for them to resist.'

'Don't sweat it, Romy. It's fine, really.'

'Really?'

'It was cathartic.'

She shot him another look and he was smiling. And she believed him. She had a feeling her parents would set a great example. If they liked you they liked you and that was that. And she knew they liked Sebastian. More than that, they adored him. And they had not so taken to a male acquaintance of hers since…well, since Liam.

Romy stopped laughing. The law student and the med student. They had been the golden couple. Until he had left her very suddenly and very publicly. And she had learned her lesson. She had learned to love carefully and privately. And then along came Sebastian. A man who took her breath away. A man whose love life was played out in the social pages of major newspapers.

He was irrepressible, gorgeous and—her mother was right—charming. And she knew that gorgeous and charming guys were, though lovely, not for her in the long run.

Then she was hit with the memory of being in Sebastian's arms, turning toward him, so close that his breath had tickled her lips. The feelings running through her veins in that moment had more than taken her breath away, they had stolen her sense, and her reason. She had never experienced their like before. Ever. Not with Liam. Not with anybody. And yet nothing had actually happened.

What if they had actually kissed? Romy was glad she was in the slow lane. Her hands had begun to shake.

She knew that sort of burning intensity was not for her in the long run. But surely she could allow herself that exhilaration one…last…time…

CHAPTER NINE

ROMY pulled up next to Sebastian's car, which he had left at her office. She turned off the engine and turned to face him, not yet ready for the night to end.

'So what do you think?'

The car stereo played softly in the background and the street lamps shone a pale glow into the car but Sebastian's face was in shadow.

'I think I am in love with your car.'

He ran a hand over the back of her seat, his fingers splaying through the soft cream sheepskin covers, tickling at her hair. Romy imagined his fingers playing across her skin in that manner and she flushed all the way to her toes.

'I mean about my parents.'

'Ah.' She could make out that he was nodding slowly. 'They're great.'

She let out a long-held breath. Apparently it mattered more than she'd thought that he liked them too. 'And their marriage?'

'Picture perfect.'

'See?' She tucked a leg beneath her. 'See how it can be. How it should be? If you really do want a family, one that will last, that is what you should be searching for.'

She felt him shuffle in his seat as he turned to face her, his profile now caught in the hazy golden glow of the street lamp. They sat mere inches apart. Their knees all but touching. Their warm breath creating a curtain of fog at the corners of the windows.

Sebastian's hand stopped moving across the back of her chair and Romy watched, transfixed, as it reached up and took a hold of a curl that rested on her shoulder. He was close. So close.

'You once told me that you thought love should be an unexpected, accelerated inferno,' she said, feeling bold under the veil of darkness. 'It should grab you by the throat and not let up for a moment as it whirls you on its relentless, ravishing ride.'

'You remembered that?'

Verbatim, she thought. 'It was…poetic.'

'So it was.'

'So, have you ever, really, experienced that kind of…sensation?' The chill was being kept at bay, outside the cocoon of the car, as

Sebastian kept her warm with his continuing caress.

'What do you think?' he asked, the height of mystery in his dark corner of the car.

'I don't know what to think.' Her mind was fast becoming numb as the sensation of his fingers brushing against her neck took over all thought.

'Is that how it is with Antony?'

He'd finally asked. She'd hoped in vain that Antony would be off limits but Sebastian had obviously reached the limit of his curiosity. His pale eyes were eerily translucent in the created light. They blinked slowly. And they watched her every minute reaction.

Her hair was tugged lightly as he wrapped and unwrapped his fingers in her curl. She knew she should pull away, but there was nothing on earth that could make her make him stop what he was doing.

'I don't think that's something you and I need to discuss,' she said on a whisper.

'Why not? If you are on a roll at showing me happy relationships, why not start even closer to home? Why not tell me all about your relationship with him?'

'Because my private life is exactly that—private.'

'Lawyer-client privilege.'

'It doesn't work that way and you know it.'

'Let's pretend it does.' Then as though reading her mind he said, 'Then tell me about Liam.'

'Why?'

'I just have the feeling he could have been your inferno.'

If you mean I was burned, she thought, *you'd be spot-on.*

'It doesn't matter,' she insisted. 'That all happened years ago.'

'Still, moments like those can change your life.'

'Hardly. I was always going to be a lawyer.'

'A divorce lawyer?'

The pause said it all. She could not remember when that decision had been made.

'The Liams of this world,' she said finally, 'the captains of the football team, the high achievers, have it too easy and thus expect all aspects of their lives to fall into place with such ease. So, though they might seem like perfect partner material, I learnt not to judge that book by its cover.'

'So no jocks, eh?' Sebastian asked, sitting before her as a prime example of the species.

'No jocks.'

'And if that's not a case of judging books by their covers I don't know what is.'

His hand unwound the curl he had been fondling and moved to her neck, the backs of his knuckles caressing her sensitive skin from the hollow of her collar-bone to the bottom of her ear. Her whole body throbbed from the attention.

Then as though the gods had planned it Dean Martin's velvet voice flowed from the stereo and Romy was undone. Sebastian was so right. And his timing was so perfect. She had to explain. Let him know it was all OK. There was no helping it; her eyes flickered closed as she gave in to the utterly new and utterly delicious sensation.

'Sebastian…'

'Yes, Romy.'

'About Antony—'

At that moment Sebastian realised he did not want to know a damn thing about Antony. Or Liam. Or any other man who thought they were enough for a woman like Romy.

She was so mellow, her hair a gilded halo about her face, the sweet, intoxicating scent of chamomile tea on her breath, her lipstick eaten away with dinner, leaving just her own sweet, soft lips to entice him. The moment was too good to miss and he knew all about missed opportunities. What he wanted at that moment was right before him and he did not need the complication of a fiancé in his way.

So he closed the space between them in one swift move and sealed that soft, waiting mouth of hers with his own. She started momentarily, and he floundered, wondering if he had misread her so very badly. Then with a soft groan that stirred against his lips she kissed him back.

It was the gentlest, sweetest yet most erotic kiss that Sebastian had ever known. Romy's sensuous lips fitted against his so completely, seducing them with their volatile, velvety softness. Even though they had continually voiced no interest in each other they had been kidding themselves. He knew that this fervent kiss had been unavoidable since they had first laid eyes on each other.

The tenderness and delicacy of the simple union of their lips stimulated the fine hairs on the back of his neck to tickle delightfully in response. He eased back, teasing, pulling ever so slightly away, and she responded with such insistent fervour it caught him off guard.

His hand at her neck dived around her back and he pulled her closer still and mutually the kiss deepened to something even more breathtaking, his insistent mouth parting and possessing her equally wanton one.

They had barely touched, barely spent time alone, barely knew anything about each other that hadn't come from a dossier, yet Sebastian was shocked to find the eagerness of the kiss was matched by equal vehemence on both their parts. What feelings. What sensations. The sense of his sense slipping away.

And then he thought of Antony.

Why now? Why when he was tumbling into a heady oblivion with this wonderful woman in his arms did he have to think of him? Why when she seemed as willing to forget his existence as he did? Problem was, Sebastian was not the bad boy everyone thought he was, so he had to pull away.

He sat back, his arms still around her as she slowly opened her eyes. They gleamed. They asked him questions he simply would not answer. There was only one way to extricate himself from her arms without smashing the delicate balance of the situation to smithereens.

'How rude of me,' he said, his voice rough with emotion. 'I seem to have cut you off mid-sentence. What were you going to say?'

What was she going to say? He expected her to remember what was in her mind five minutes before? Before he'd obliterated all authentic thought within the radius of her car.

She backed away, slowly extricating herself from his warm embrace. She ran a hand through her tumble of curls, as though neatening them would put her life back in order.

He was smiling at her so kindly, a glint in his eye, calmly waiting for her to respond. But her mind was as opaque as the foggy windows.

Anyone outside would think they had been parking like a couple of teenagers. Her mind pushed back a few moments and she recalled in vivid playback that was exactly what they had been doing.

'Romy?'

She clicked back to the present. 'I'm sure it doesn't matter. You…you should probably go.'

'I should probably have gone ten minutes ago.'

'Mmm.' But it had been so nice. And though her world might very well crumble into unfixable pieces at her feet, she would not have given up that kiss for anything.

Sebastian leaned over, turned on the demister and instantly the foggy windows began to clear. Romy drank in his scent, warm, engaging and so very male. Sebastian then opened the car door, letting in a rush of night air, and the scent was gone, leaving just icy chill and emptiness. He eased out of the car and leant in for one last moment.

'Thanks for tonight's lesson.'

Romy simply stared. What on earth…?

'Your parents were a great example to us all.'

'Oh, of course.' *Of course.*

'Shall I pick you up at your place?'

She blinked.

'Tomorrow? Sanctuary Cove?'

The golf trip. With the firm's partners. She had never been invited before. But that meant she would be alone with Sebastian. Away from home. Away from stability. So much for one…last…time. Would the pleasure of one heavenly kiss be enough or would his proximity mean she would want to relive the experience?

She shook her head. 'No. I don't think I can—'

'Don't be silly. This is your chance to mix it up with the big boys.' He placed a finger beneath her chin and lifted her face so she would look him in the eye. 'Who knows, maybe you can find me a little golf groupie? Or a caddy? Or the girl who puts the chocolates on the pillows at night? How would the papers like that one, do you think? They met on a golf course… Poetic, don't you think? Join my two media miseries; golf and women.'

'Sebastian—'

'Go home. Early to bed. I'll be at your place bright and early in the morning.'

He closed the door with a soft click. Alone with her heavy breathing, the whirring demister and Dean Martin she came back down to earth.

What had she done? The day Antony came back to town and she had thrown herself into the path of another man. True, she and Antony had no claim on each other until her decision had been made, but still…

She ran a finger over her bruised lips; the imprint of him was still so fresh. Sebastian had once joked that he was damaged and she now knew it to be true. And she just knew she could heal him. But just because she could, did that mean that she should? Even if it meant she would play further into the man's hands and away from all she had so carefully built for herself?

But she had to admit Sebastian was not just another man. He was a person who touched her soul. He made her want to laugh and cry at once just by being him. And for a girl who did not enjoy surprises, his innate goodness was the biggest one of all.

And she loved him for it.

She clapped a hand over her mouth as though she had said those words aloud. She didn't love Sebastian! What was she thinking? She barely even liked him, right?

But why else would she be so willing to throw her carefully constructed life away unless it was to put everything on the line for that greatest of possibilities…love?

The windows had half cleared and Romy watched as his long, easy strides took him to his car. She had to admit Gloria was right; no matter the trillion other features and benefits the guy had going for him, it was sure nice to watch him walk away.

Half an hour later, in the long ride up in the lift to her apartment, Romy was glad for the creaking and groaning that accompanied its slow progress. She was glad she had fought the tenants group to have the lift restored and not replaced. A new lift would have come with accompanying elevator music and knowing her luck it would have been the best of Dean Martin.

She had one message on her machine. The voice caught at her chest as soon as the low strains reached her ears. Her hand moved to cover her stomach as if that could stop what felt like an imminent collapse.

'Romy, it's Sebastian. If you've got the paper napkin on you, I have another quality you can add to the non-negotiable list.' He paused and she felt her life tumble over on itself in that silence. 'She must drink chamomile tea. I didn't know what I was missing.'

The machine clicked and whirred and reset itself.

Romy slumped onto her chair as the knowledge ran through her head that Sebastian had not drunk chamomile tea. Only she had.

How could she deny how he affected her? With a voice so sensual it made her feel as if she was coming down with the flu. Her head throbbed, she had a heightened temperature, weak knees, clammy hands, shortness of breath.

That was it. That was the final proof. Either the guy was hazardous to her health or she was head over heels in love. More likely, it would turn out to both.

The next morning, by quarter-past five Romy was ready. When Sebastian rang the bell she was sitting on her overnight bag, biting the last of her fingernails to shreds and tapping one foot against the floor so hard it was beginning to ache. She whipped the door open and dragged her bag outside and towards the lift before he had a chance to make chit-chat.

Her plan for the day and night was to keep up the pace. No time to think. No time to analyse. Just go go go. Network. Get as much out of the professional opportunities as she could. And if Sebastian was to be the key to unlocking the door to the partners' washroom, so be it.

'Are we in any particular hurry?' Sebastian asked.

She turned to find him still standing at her door, arms outstretched. Fresh as a daisy. His hair was natural, spiky, raked back by his fingers. The black T-shirt he wore fit firm to his muscular chest. His biceps strained against the soft cotton. He wore aged denim jeans, washed over and over again until they fitted like a glove, hugging every robust curve. He was so virile it ached.

It's lust! Not love, she determined in a pathetic attempt to convince herself. What had she been thinking? The guy was a perennial playboy. He probably kissed a different girl every night, she thought, and as such their effort in the car park was probably a regular Thursday night for him. But nevertheless it was as though she had succumbed to the possibility of him. The potential inside the man. And the makeover had barely begun!

Now the way he looked at her, with such knowledge in his eyes, she suddenly wondered if she had zipped her top all the way up and had to check that her shoes matched. No wonder women threw themselves at him. The package was just too tempting.

It was certainly a perfectly reasonable excuse for letting him kiss her the night before. At least once in a woman's lifetime she should be allowed to sample such a treat. But once it had to be. A girl needed her sleep and any more encounters like that would turn her into a raging…insomniac!

'I thought I could at least score a grand tour,' he said, his voice so smooth and engaging.

She repeatedly jabbed at the down button outside the elevator. 'The only thing you'll score in the next day will be a golf score.'

Romy clamped a hand over her runaway mouth. Where on earth had that come from? Sebastian held his ground. Then slowly a grin broke out across his lovely face. It was a winner's grin. It was a grin that knocked the breath from Romy's already tight lungs.

'Please come on. Let's just go.'

Sebastian lifted his feet and slowly swaggered towards her. Romy begged the gods to make the lift hurry. For once in its old life. But no, it creaked and groaned from many floors below.

'Is something on your mind, Romy?'

'Nope. Not a thing. Just preparing myself for the big game. Just readying myself to beat the pants off you.'

What? She snapped her eyes closed and hung her head, shaking it back and forth, willing her jaw to clamp shut. She felt rather than saw him stand behind her.

'No matter your renowned skills, I'm not sure that you are quite ready for that yet,' he said.

Her eyes flung open and she stared at her tapping shoes.

'I mean,' he said, 'we were interrupted yesterday before I got the chance to really improve your stroke. But if you would care to go back inside your apartment—'

The elevator pinged and Romy almost collapsed under the weight of her relief. The last thing she needed was for her big mouth to tell him that she'd had no complaints about her stroke in the past.

She ripped the mesh door open and rushed in, keeping far to one side of the small cage. Sebastian sauntered in after her and she slammed the door shut. She pressed the button for the ground floor. Not once but several times.

The lift took off. Slowly. Grunting and groaning.

'Will this rusty thing make it, do you think?' Sebastian asked.

'It's not rusty. It's antique. Solid. Dependable.'

'I see. And so being dependable is high on your list of non-negotiables. For an apartment building, I mean.'

Romy stiffened. She knew exactly what he meant. And maybe now was the time for that conversation after all.

'Of course. Dependability is extremely important. An apartment building should have a good history. It should be stable. Comfortable. No trouble.'

'And this apartment? How has it been treating you?'

As the lift reached the bottom floor it gave a great hulking groan to show just how much trouble it had the capacity to cause. Romy opened the doors and waited for Sebastian to pass her by. She shot him a warning glance. 'It hasn't disappointed me yet.'

He turned and faced her, he outside the lift, she inside. He looked deep into her eyes and the world stood still. Romy felt as though whatever happened next could change everything. And she had to fight the urge to slam the gate shut, flee into her cosy apartment and switch the lights off. She stood with her hands gripping the edge of the door. Waiting.

'Just let go.'

Let go. Of what? Of security. Of simplicity. And give in to him and all that his voice and his look and his reputation seemed to promise?

'Come on, crazy lady. Let go of the door before it closes in on you.' He reached over and took her by the arm, leading her through the lobby and out into the uncertain twilight.

CHAPTER TEN

SEBASTIAN helped Romy into the cab he had hired to take them to the airport. In the place of sexy black suits and killer high heels she wore a bright blue zip-up top over plush pink stretch trousers patterned in random blue daisies. The top made her bright eyes pop, and the trousers hugged every delicious curve of her delectably rounded behind and down her long, lithe legs.

Her hair was long and straight, not quite up to its usual perfect standard, her face was still soft from late deep sleep, and she looked just wonderful. All that heavy blinking as she tried to stifle her dozen or so yawns was hypnotic.

If he had been hoping the night apart would make their kiss seem like some kind of not to be repeated dream, he had been kidding himself. Seeing her soft lips made up in the barest hint of shimmering gloss made the kiss achingly real. She was skittish as a kitten and he couldn't take his eyes off her.

But she could not look him in the eye. If that kiss had meant she was prepared to take their undeniable attraction to the next level, surely she would have been more receptive. Would have given him some sign that it meant as much to her as it did to him. But she looked on the verge of a nervous breakdown.

And he knew why. She felt as guilty as hell and it was all his fault. He knew she was taken and had pushed her into that kiss anyway. So it would be up to him to swallow his intense reactions to her and give it up. At least he should try.

'So, Ms Bridgeport. How is the project going compared with your original plans?'

She leapt as though he had jolted her with a fire poker. 'Sorry?'

'My makeover? Our little project? Your ambition to mould me into model marriage material?'

She blinked. 'It's not going exactly to plan,' she admitted. It was enough to make him think of switching tack and grabbing her in his arms and kissing until she forgot any other men even existed outside of their cab but she clammed up and turned back to watch the uninspiring motorway walls whip past.

'Well, just think of the next two days as an opportunity to get it back on track.'

She slowly turned to face him. 'Really?'

Yeah, really? Is that what he really wanted? For her to be telling him what she thought made a perfect partner and then for him to become exactly that? *And then* have to turn it on for someone else? But by the look of desperation on her lovely face he knew that was *exactly* what *she* wanted.

'Sure,' he finally said. 'Of course. Remember the caddy? Or the girl who puts the chocolates on the pillows at night? If I am to be ready for them I will need your help.'

She nodded, seeming to gain a modicum of strength from the thought.

'Or perhaps there might even be someone from your office who is looking to leave all that nasty law stuff behind to become a wife and mother.'

She stopped nodding quick smart. Why had he said that? To provoke her into some sort of reaction other than this unnerving silent panic? To provoke her into a fit of jealous rage? Why not?

'Would you make your wife quit her job to spawn your children?' she seethed, her face gaining some much-needed colour. But her outrage made Sebastian feel much more comfortable than her trepidation. Though the response he had to that flash in her eyes was anything but comfortable.

'If that was what she wanted to do.'

She glared at him, obviously unsure of which insinuation was serious.

'You are such a hard taskmaster, Romy. I don't know what to do about you.'

'I am a perfectionist, that's all. I don't see what's so wrong about trying to make the best of your life.'

'Neither do I. But people make mistakes. That's the way it goes. You have to forgive and move on. Being so perfect is not what it's all about. Don't be so hard on your clients, don't be so hard on me and especially don't be so hard on yourself.'

She stared back at him as though nobody had ever spoken to her in this way before. Well, maybe they hadn't. And she sure needed it.

'Forgive Liam. Forgive your clients. Forgive me. Nobody's perfect, we're just all muddling along trying our best to reach our goals whilst hurting as few people along the way as possible. So take a chance. Trust somebody other than yourself.'

* * *

Trust? Romy thought, glancing back out the window to watch the cars speed through the early-morning traffic. *I don't have a problem with trust. I simply have learnt to trust only those who have not let me down.*

She wanted to be prepared, she wanted to be ready, and she would seek out a relationship exactly like the one her parents had. A relationship bound in trust.

She suddenly thought of Libby Gold and wondered how her dinner with Jeffrey had gone. There was a woman with a boundless capacity to forgive and Romy felt a jab of envy as she realised she had nowhere near that much mercy in her. But was it as easy as Sebastian made out? Was letting go and trusting someone else all it took?

She dragged her eyes away from the drizzly scene outside to glance his way. Though she could have sworn he had been staring at her for the longest time, he was looking forward, gazing calmly past the back of the driver's head and out the front window.

He had such a glorious profile. Straight nose, strong brow, smoky grey-green eyes framed by the most unfairly luscious lashes. And the most perfectly carved pair of lips. Lips that despite all preconceptions spoke only of fidelity and honesty. Lips that smiled so easily. Lips that less than twelve hours before she had kissed. And had those lips just intimated that she should close her eyes, let go and trust him?

Of anything that had been said and done between them that frightened her more than the other things combined.

They made it to the airport in plenty of time and found themselves soon swallowed into the burgeoning group of seriously excited lawyers and top clients. A fifty-seater commuter plane had been booked and filled by the firm.

Sebastian was the star of the day and Romy was quite happy to let him be taken away by his group of fans. She had enough to think about without having the subject of her thoughts standing by her, smelling so good, helping her through doorways, being so darned trustworthy.

Sebastian was on the plane first and as Romy approached she swung her gaze around for someone to sit with. Someone else.

And then Sebastian called her over, offering her the window seat he had saved for her and she almost collapsed. Any earlier in their acquaintance and she would have thought he had bribed Gloria for that sort of information. But she knew better. She knew that was just him. Polite, thoughtful him.

And she wondered briefly if Antony would give up his window seat for her. And she knew without a doubt he would happily describe the view in minute detail without offering her the chance to experience it herself. With Antony it was like watching life go by. In Sebastian's company she lived every second in surround sound and Technicolor.

And why on earth was she comparing the two? Their positions in her life were entirely separate issues. It was not as though she had ever considered Sebastian marriage material. Not for her anyway.

Romy had her mouth open, trying to find some excuse not to be alone with him—alone with fifty other people and she was still anxious—when she felt a tap on her shoulder.

'You must be "Womy" of the troll and ogre fame.'

Romy turned to face Bridget, the only woman partner in the firm. 'Um, yep. That's me.'

'I belong to the twins. They adore you. Though I have to complain that, since you came along, Mum's stories just don't cut it. Looking for a seat?'

Romy was still slack-jawed. 'Um, sure.'

'Great. You can come and play with me. If I have to sit in on another two-hour conversation about graphite wedges and nine irons I think I will throw myself from the plane.'

Bridget took Romy by the arm and led her towards the front of the aircraft. Romy shot a quick apologetic glance over her shoulder but she had the feeling Sebastian knew she was less sorry than she made out.

'So,' Bridget began once they had settled in and the plane engines began to rumble, 'I see you have brought our star client along for the weekend. Well done.'

By the twinkle in Bridget's eye Romy was not quite sure that the 'well done' was entirely professionally based.

'I promise you, it is our star client who brought me along for the weekend.'

That earned her a raised eyebrow.

'I mean I have never been invited to one of these junkets before. I think I was asked along as little more than a babysitter.'

'Don't be silly. To get a spot on this plane you have to have earned it. Gerard is not one to give away a seat impulsively. If you are here it is because he believes you deserve to be here.'

Bridget shot her an appraising look. 'Do you not think you deserve to be here?'

'I always thought I deserved to be here. Even before *our star client* came along.'

Bridget nodded and seemed more than happy with that answer. 'Beware though, by the end of the weekend you might very well wish you have never been invited.'

'Why?'

'Unless you have a stomach of iron and need less than four hours sleep a night, by Sunday you will be toast. A quivering, exhausted lump of toast.'

Romy could do little but smile as she had no idea what Bridget could possibly mean by that strange analogy.

Having blithely moved on from her disturbing warning, Bridget motioned towards the back of the plane and Romy felt she should glance back as well. 'Seems he's quite the popular fellow.'

Romy started when she saw that Sebastian was now seated with Jennifer, Gerard's predatory young assistant. Her heart slammed into her ribcage with such force she had to gulp down her next breath. And when she turned back she saw the twinkle had only brightened in Bridget's eye.

'Now, tell me where you get your hair done. It is absolutely the most glorious cut!' And Romy and Bridget spent the remainder of the flight focusing on purely feminine pursuits, thankfully none of which included talk of men.

Sebastian dragged his attention from the back of Romy's animated head to the woman at his side. Jennifer somebody? Gerard's assistant. She seemed to know all about him and his move to the firm. And she also seemed to need things from the bag between her feet a good deal, which meant she was constantly rubbing her knee against his and affording him glimpses of her ample chest.

She was a doll. Brunette. Confident. Voracious. No harm in chatting. After all, if Romy wasn't there to assist him on their project, he might as well go it alone.

'Have you worked for the firm for long?' he asked.

'A couple of years. Gerard took me from the typing pool. I give great dictation.'

Sebastian all but choked on his drink. 'I don't doubt that.'

The woman took a long sip of her cooler. 'So I hear that Romy Bridgeport's beau Antony Lucas is in town.'

Sebastian swung his gaze back to his companion. That was some leap in topic. 'You heard right.'

She smiled knowingly. 'He's a shark, that one. Real up-and-comer. Rumour is he proposed the last time he was in town. And rumour is that this time he is back for his answer.'

Sebastian's glass stopped halfway to his mouth. Back for his answer? Did that mean Romy wasn't engaged? No matter the welcome back the lucky guy had received, had she really not yet accepted his proposal? Was that why there was no ring? Was that why she had leapt so readily into his arms in her car the other night? Was he a testing ground for her answer? Did he care? No. He didn't. Not if it meant that her answer could very well depend upon him.

Jennifer was watching him very carefully and he knew she was taking note of every pause, every grimace, every eyelid flutter, all of which would no doubt be reported back to the typing pool. He brought the glass to his mouth and took a measured sip.

'Do you pay that much attention to rumours, Jennifer?'

'They do tend to be true, Sebastian.'

She could very well have been right.

* * *

Romy and Bridget only had carry-on luggage so headed straight for the bank of drivers awaiting them at Brisbane Airport. Bridget had a tight hold of her, obviously assuming they would catch a limo together. They were halfway through a conversation about Bridget's twelve-year-old son, who was staying with cousins as her ex-husband was too unreliable to take him on even for a couple of days, and Bridget had nowhere near finished ranting.

Romy's attention was hooked. An idea was fast forming in her mind and she suddenly wished she was back in her office with Gloria at the other end of a 2B pencil writing it all down.

'Hey,' Bridget said, 'am I right in thinking you came up with the divorced-singles dating club we have going on Tuesday nights?'

Romy tucked her idea to the back of her mind for later. 'You are. And it's been a great success. Several of my latest clients have come on board with the firm only after hearing of the programme.'

Bridget shook her head in amazement. 'You are one innovative lady. No wonder Gerard bade me go chat to you on the plane trip.'

Romy's head almost burst with pride. Gerard had asked Bridget to seek her out? Did that mean he had really had his eye on her before Sebastian had burst on to the scene? Though, for all the trouble Sebastian had caused, she had to admit he opened doors that she had only managed to unlock.

'I do what I can to make the transition as easy as possible,' she said, trying to keep the delight from her voice. 'I think we owe our clients that.'

'And it also makes me wonder if you are so *hands-on* with all of your clients.' Again that twinkle was back in her eye and Romy had to use all of her strength to halt a telling blush.

The two of them sprinted to the first car, hurrying to avoid the sudden sun shower.

Romy brushed the water droplets from her hair as they took off. The car slowed as it reached a bottleneck at the end of the line and Romy caught a long glimpse of Sebastian getting into a car with Jennifer. And her heart leapt to her throat. They looked very chummy, gathered together under an umbrella. Talk about hands-on. Jennifer clamped on to his arm, and her bag as well as his own was thrown over his shoulder.

But by then it was too late. They would be spending over an hour in the back of a limo together. She should be thrilled he was putting himself out there. And Romy was sure Jennifer would fit into his non-negotiables list just fine. So what did she have to complain about?

Antony was back. She had two days to make up her mind for good. And those two days would be spent in the company of the one man who had managed to wrench her from her comfortable cocoon and make her think that the choice was there for the making.

She could hardly complain that the trip was not going according to any sort of plan. This whole event was so far beyond her plans she felt as if for the first time in years that her time was in fate's hand, and not hers. And it scared her silly.

Within the hour they were on the golf course, and naturally she had been partnered with Sebastian for the opening round of the game. She knew Gerard's maxim that she should 'keep him on a short leash' would be put to the test that weekend, but still the sight of Sebastian in his tweed trousers, butter-yellow polo shirt and caramel golf shoes was heart-stopping. He looked the epitome of the dashing young sportsman. He would have cut a fine sight on the pro tour. And again she wondered what had made him stop.

CHAPTER ELEVEN

THE flight had not eased Romy's tension; if anything she seemed more uptight as she walked towards him in her bright garb. She had changed into bright blue golf shoes. He had no idea where anyone could find golf shoes of that colour, but golf shoes they were. The woman was a wonder. Though he knew without a doubt she was as nervous as hell amongst the big boys, she certainly had no intention of letting anyone forget she was there that day.

Only once the game was underway did Romy seem to believe she was there to play and not to run the drinks cart. She twirled her mass of hair into a makeshift pony-tail and tucked it under a pink cap. She pulled out a leather glove, picked the dead right golf club, set herself up, wiggled her behind and smacked that ball for all it was worth.

'Nice shot!' he said, shielding his eyes from the late-morning sun with a cupped palm, as he watched the ball glide in a perfect arc down the fairway.

She glanced his way, and could not keep the pleasure from her vibrant blue eyes. 'What did you expect?'

'Nothing less,' he admitted. 'Your dad said you were good and he was right. Unless of course that was a complete fluke.'

She narrowed her eyes at Sebastian as he lined up his shot. He took a deep breath, drinking in the glorious familiar scent of freshly cut grass and recent rain. He shut out the noise of the neighbourhood traffic, the chatter of people laughing at a nearby hole, the breeze playing through the line of trees at his side.

The only thing he could not block out was the image of Romy leaning on her golf club, watching him with such intensity. The image was burned on his mind as he shifted his feet. He ran his finger a little lower on the leather grip of the club and remembered the feel of Romy's body against his as he had pretended to fix her perfect grip on a broom handle. He cleared his throat and straightened.

'What's the matter?' she asked, her voice brimming with delight. 'Scared of being beaten by a girl?'

He could not help but laugh. She knew he had been a pro and still she had every intention of showing she could do it better. He could feel her grin. If only she knew what had stopped him she would not be grinning. He suddenly ached to tell her exactly what was blocking his concentration but they had a couple of days to get through in each other's pockets. A couple of days and a night.

He lined up once more, and hoped his natural instincts would make him at least able to connect with the small white ball. He fixed his grip, swung and with a hearty smack the ball sailed through the air. They watched in silence as it finally hit the ground a good thirty metres ahead of Romy's ball. He smiled.

'Not scared. Just thinking that instead of you beating the pants off me I would very much enjoy it being the other way around.' He gave her pink trousers the once-over and before she could throw her heavy club in his direction he grabbed his cart and took off down the fairway, whistling contentedly.

'So if you are such an advocate for marriage, why didn't you become, say, a marriage counsellor?' he asked over his shoulder.

He heard her feet pad up behind him. 'Oh, no. The fight's all gone by then. When it reaches the stage of divorce, it means the embers of passion have been sparked once more and with that sort of focus it means they finally know what they really want and need. And they are ready to go out there and fight for it.'

She had a point. When he had spilled his desire for a family to her that night, he had spoken the truth. He had so known what he wanted he could almost taste it. And now he knew it tasted like chamomile tea.

They set their golf clubs down and Romy picked out an iron. 'Why did you take up golf?' she asked.

'I can't remember exactly why or when. I was always pretty athletic at school. I guess that came from living in such a rambunctious household. There was always some game or another going on in the back yard.'

'And you were captain of the football team, I bet.'

Like Liam, he remembered, the boy who had broken her heart. She did not need to say it. The pain in her response had been palpable. But it was a pain he had not seen before. He had seen regret, disappointment, embarrassment even, but not such raw pain. Such new pain.

She lined up the ball and it seemed she could no longer look him in the eye. And then it hit him. The panic in her hallway. The sudden shy glances. The desperate relief at not having to sit with him in the plane. She liked him a good deal more than she cared to admit.

Something was holding her back and he somehow thought that, though a flesh and blood guy, Antony was little more than the excuse he had originally thought him to be. Did he remind her of the one who had broken her heart? Did he remind her of someone with whom she had once been very much in love? Sebastian had to lean on his clubs so as not to fall over backwards.

'Not captain. I also played baseball and cricket and was on the swimming team. So was never really committed enough to one to be considered captain material. Once I finished college I stopped playing all the other sports regularly but golf stayed with me. I loved hitting the green at sun-up. I could take the same path the birds took to follow the warmth. I could watch the grass move as it angled towards the rising sun. It was as though the world was waking up around me.'

He kept his eyes on his feet as he stubbed a leather-covered toe at a divot, softly pressing it back into place.

'It seems a bit of a pattern with me. I flounder a bit until I find where I am meant to be and then I flourish.'

He shot Romy a glance but she had her back to him. She set herself up, did her all too enticing bottom wiggle and hit the ball. This time she sliced it badly and it ended up bouncing into the shrubs at the edge of the fairway.

'Oops.' She turned to him with a blush he was sure was not entirely embarrassment. 'Best two of three?'

'Not on your sweet life. You hit that one fair and square so you play it from where it lands.' Sebastian grabbed a hold of both Romy's golf bag and his own and made the trek towards her ball so she had no choice but to follow.

'So why did you *stop* playing golf?' she asked. It had never come up in her research, it hadn't seemed important. But now it did. Now it seemed the most important question she had ever asked of him.

He shrugged. 'Injured my back. It was stop playing so much or risk my health.'

'How did you injure your back?' she asked. The information must have been buried deep in his dossier but she could not remember the details.

'Car accident.' The look he shot her beneath his lashes was not happy.

She knew there was more to it than that but sensed now was not the time or place. So she left it at that. She grabbed any old club and headed off into the bushes. She tried to concentrate on finding her ball but her mind was spinning a million miles a minute. She felt as if she was coming to some grand conclusion. As if the pieces of the Sebastian puzzle were so close to fitting. But the gap left by that missing piece let bright daylight shine through, blinding her to the whole.

She found her ball and stabbed at it with enough finesse to send it back to the fairway and skimming ahead of Sebastian's ball. She climbed over shrubs and scratchy grass to join Sebastian there. He was standing still. Watching her with an intensity that unsettled her.

'So, what do you think of Jennifer?' Sebastian asked out of the blue.

Manipulative. Forward. A man-eater.

'Jennifer? Gerard's assistant, Jennifer?' she asked.

'Hmm. I sat next to her on the plane. Nice girl. Great…conversationalist. And the first woman I have seriously flirted with since we started on our crusade. So,' he repeated, 'do you think she would be a likely candidate?'

Likely if all you are looking for is another avenue for alimony.

'What does it matter what I think? Remember, finding you a girl is not in my job description. Getting you ready to take the leap seriously is my only guideline.'

'And if I'm ready?'

His voice had lowered, softened, drifted to her on a spine-tingling whisper. Or was it her imagination?

'Well, she fits into your list criteria perfectly.'

And has little else to offer, from what I've seen.

Sebastian seemed to think for a moment before laughing. 'That she does.'

'But you have to remember there's more to a relationship than an intractable wish list.'

'Such as?'

She glanced at him. Was he really serious? About *Jennifer*? Or was he baiting her? Was he trying to get her to divulge something? His expression was all innocence. 'Such as, does she make your heart race when you look upon her?'

As mine does when I even think about you.

She felt her voice rising to an unnecessarily shrill level, but she could not stop herself. 'Can you see her as the mother of your children?'

As I see you with mine; in three-legged races, bandaging grazed knees, and rocking them to sleep.

Oh, hell! It was all true. Her dreams had gone from sexual fantasies to happy families and were all the more dangerous for it!

Romy fought the urge to retract her question. But Sebastian's eyes narrowed and for a split-second Romy thought she had been sprung, and for the first time in her life she knew what they meant when they talked about a person's heart being on their shoulder. She felt as though hers was pounding there, like a heavy weight with an arrow straight through the middle with Sebastian's name on it.

But then he surprised her by asking, 'As you can see Antony as the father of your children?'

The big Sebastian arrow was torn from her heavy pumping heart and it deflated to a quivering mess at her muddy feet.

Antony. How on earth could she explain to Sebastian about Antony? Kind, sweet, patient Antony. Antony, whom she had dated sporadically over the last few years. Antony, who was a complete gentleman who had never asked more of her than a goodnight kiss. Antony, who, at the very moment she realised he would be perfect husband material, had proposed. She had asked him to give her a month to decide and he had. At the time she had simply added another gold star to his name for his patience and humility but now the image raged in her mind.

He had not even argued. He had not landed on one knee and begged her to choose him then and there or he would be lost forever. And he had not said he loved her. But then again if she loved him, why would she have needed a month to decide?

She imagined Sebastian proposing and just knew it would take her less than a heartbeat to decide. She felt as though she had taken ten steps backwards. She was not meant to feel like this about someone like Sebastian. But the problem was she had never felt this way about anyone else.

'Romy?' Sebastian touched her shoulder, his thumb brushing along the bare skin at her collar-bone, the warmth of his strong fingertips melting along her arm. His voice was soft and low and gave her the unfamiliar urge to spill her soul. After the encounter they had shared the night before, if he wanted to know about Antony she would tell him.

'Sebastian, I—'

'The beer's here!' Gerard called out as he and a couple of his cronies trundled up to them on a golf cart laden with beer cans and munchies. 'Whose shot is it? Sebastian? OK, on this hole, shortest shot downs one beer and longest shot downs two.'

Sebastian's hand left her and her gumption seeped away with it. She watched as though from far away as Sebastian lined up and swung at the ball, every sinew in his body lining up perfectly to create his graceful, perfect form. The ball landed on the green and curved to a halt a couple of metres from the flag.

Romy lined up for hers and swung, and though this time it was straight it missed the green by several metres. The guys on the golf buggy cheered nevertheless as they passed out the allocated beers. Romy looked to Sebastian for help but he just popped open the drink with a distinct click and a swish as cool gas escaped the can. He passed it to her and grabbed another two for himself.

'Drink up, Romy,' Gerard insisted. 'There's another crew breathing down your neck. So down your drink and on you move. Chop-chop.'

Romy suddenly understood Bridget's warning. This was going to be a long weekend! She brought the can to her lips and took a large gulp of the bubbly drink. It was cold and bitter and better suited to a midsummer's day barbecue.

'Thanks, Gerard,' Sebastian said, a huge grin on his face. 'I'll make sure these are looked after properly.'

Gerard looked from one to the other and, seeming satisfied, shot them a hearty salute and sped off to meet the next couple along the line.

'Thank heaven they're gone!' Romy gushed. 'Should we tip them out here or in the bushes?'

Sebastian raised one telling eyebrow. 'You're not planning on dismissing the rules, are you? Wouldn't that mean chaos?'

'I didn't come here in order to drink myself into stumbling into a water hazard.'

'So why did you come?'

Because you asked me to. Because any opportunity to spend time with you is too precious to deny. Because I have crossed my own unwritten line and fallen for you.

'Because this is a fabulous opportunity to spend time with those higher up in the firm. With those whose choice it is to make me partner.'

'Oh. You see, I thought you were here to keep me happy. Isn't that what Gerard told you to do once I left your staff meeting yesterday?'

She glared at him. 'And what if it is?'

'Well. Why don't you ask what would make me happy?'

The corners of his alluring mouth were twitching into the beginnings of a satisfied smile. If at that moment he asked her to run into the bushes with him she would have beaten him there. She felt her cheeks burning. But she was infinitely glad that he was still grinning. It meant he had no idea what she was going through, standing there, miles from home with a golf club in one hand and a beer in the other. Talk about her life not going to plan!

She swallowed hard and asked, 'What would make you happy, Sebastian?'

'We play golf. We drink beer. And I win.'

Romy breathed out a ragged sigh of relief. Well, it was not in her to deliberately lose in order to make him happy. Then it dawned on her—whereas before she stood very little chance of beating him, with Gerard's rules in place, suddenly the idea of whipping him on the course seemed possible.

She held up her beer in salute. 'Fine. We play. We drink. And may the best person win.'

By five o'clock they were back in the hotel and Romy was smashed.

'I cannot handle another day of this,' Romy sulked groggily as she trudged into her room, draped all over Sebastian. He led her over to her bed, which was covered in a gaudy seashell bed-spread. Once she was within slumping distance, she let go and slumped, face down, spread-eagled, onto the bed. Once he was sure she would not fall off, he took a few steps back.

'Well, you are going to have to do it all again,' he said. 'Our flight home is not until tomorrow night.'

She lifted her heavy head and dragged off the three medallions she had been awarded.

'What was this one for?' she asked, her arm wavering as she held them out to him. He hesitated a moment before coming close enough to snatch them away. 'This one was for the highest number of shots over par on the thirteenth hole. This one was for landing in the most number of sand traps. And the third was for something you would rather not remember. But I have a feeling it will be relived over and over again by the staff when you go back to work.'

She groaned. 'Please don't make me go out there again. I don't care if they demote me to junior associate and make me work from a broom cupboard in the archives room, I cannot do that again for a minute, much less a whole day.'

'OK.'

She peeled her flushed face from the bed and he saw the bedcover had already left a slight imprint in her soft skin. She shot him the most heart-wrenching, sexy smile. 'OK?'

'I have a better idea of what we can do instead.'

Her brows furrowed but that seemed to hurt her thumping head even more so she slowly smoothed it out again.

'We are only a couple of hours' drive from my beach house. I can get a driver from the hotel to take us down there tonight and we can have a glorious, relaxing day in Byron Bay tomorrow instead.'

'Why on earth would you want to show me your beach house?' Romy asked, her wary voice telling him of her trepidation more than a furrowed brow ever could.

'Because it's where I grew up.'

She sprang up onto her knees as if she had been hit with lightning. 'You mean your foster home? With all the kids?'

'The very one.'

'But when did you…? How did you…?'

'The Gibsons passed on several years ago, within about six months of one another, and still owed a lot of money on the house. They spent every spare cent on the kids for so long, the home was mortgaged up to its gables. I found out a couple of years later and it was empty, the bank having simply let it go. So I bought it, did it up and I spend as much time there as I can; swimming, fishing, four-wheel driving.'

She looked at him with the maudlin sadness that came with too many drinks. 'So you really have nobody.' Her voice was a wavering whisper.

'Not at all. I have my sister and her three kids.'

'But no parents. No foster parents. No wives. No wonder you are such an easy catch. Lonely man. They all seem to leave you.' Her fuzzy brain then caught up with her tongue and she slapped a hand over her wayward mouth. 'I'm so sorry. I didn't mean it like that, I just meant…'

He shrugged. It was all true. 'It's OK.'

'No. No, I just meant that it shouldn't have ever happened to a man like you. You're so…good and selfless and…extraordinary. I would bet my life on the fact that you've never done anything to deserve all the bad luck.'

She was still looking up at him, her big blue eyes staring into his with not a hint of the usual wariness, or reticence or self-chastisement. She was looking at him with such tenderness. It had to be the drink. It took all of his determination not to take those two steps back to the bed and take advantage of her weak state and kiss the adorable expression from her luscious mouth.

'What about Jennifer?' she finally asked.

'Who?'

'Your plane date,' she sulked and his spirits lifted another foot closer to the ceiling. Oh, Jennifer. He hadn't thought about her once since asking Romy about her on the course.

'I don't think we need to invite Jennifer.'

She seemed satisfied by that. 'Is it really only a couple of hours' drive?'

'Mm-hmm. And the bedrooms are already made up; there's a store cupboard and freezer fully stocked.

'Do you think Gerard will be angry?' she whispered as though he might be standing outside the door, listening.

'Not at all. I will explain that we have some work to do on our special project and he will be just fine.'

She nodded as though coming to some sort of conclusion. 'I would be honoured to see the house where you grew up, but I'll only come on one condition.'

'Name it.'

'No drinking games.'

That brought a smile to his face. 'You've got it.'

CHAPTER TWELVE

THREE hours later, the driver angled his luxury sedan around the rest of the circular driveway and drove away, leaving Romy and Sebastian standing on the front porch, their luggage in hand. That, along with the fresh sting of salty sea air washing in from the nearby coast, was enough to sober Romy up quick smart.

What on earth was she doing there? Outside a big old empty house. Alone. With Sebastian. Well, it was too late now. Unless she had it in her to sprint down the dark road after the car, she was stuck.

Sebastian was standing on the threshold. 'Are you coming in or do you plan on turning into an icicle out here?'

'I'm coming. I was just enjoying the…clear night sky.' Her gaze swept from his unreadable face and skyward. Her breath caught in her throat. There was a clear night sky all right. Miles away from city lights the Milky Way swept across the velvety black heavens.

'It's quite a view isn't it?' Sebastian's voice was unnaturally husky and Romy found him still looking straight at her. His face was hooded in the shadows under the porch, whereas Romy felt herself glowing in the light spilling across the ground from the unhindered moon. And the last thing she wanted was for Sebastian to see her, to really see what she was feeling.

He was trying to find his feet. The last thing he needed was for yet another eager woman to promise to ease his loneliness. He needed this time on his own, bettering himself, expelling his demons, so that when the time was right he would have every chance at real happiness for the first time in his adult life.

'You're right,' she said, her voice overly bright, 'it's freezing out here. When you said beach house I pictured warm, summery nights.'

Sebastian ushered her inside and she had to brush against his length to pass by. He held up an arm at the last minute, trapping her in the small space afforded by the doorway. 'Come back in summer,' he said, 'and I'll see what I can do.'

Her heart beat in her throat but she knew she could not give in to the sensations raging through her trapped body. It was time to set some ground rules.

'Sebastian, by summer I hope you will be happily married and I…' She faltered, having been trapped again, this time by her own hubris.

'And you?' Sebastian asked, so close his breath tickled her fringe.

What would her situation be by summer? That was something she had to decide by the end of the weekend and she was darn well not going to decide it whilst standing in the moonlight, flush against this guy.

'I will finally be rid of you and working overtime playing catch-up with my other clients.'

'Hmm.' He released his arm and Romy all but bolted through the door and into Sebastian's beach house.

She was hit with the instant feeling of family. The split-level home was expansive yet still cosy. She could feel the happy memories tripping across the polished wood floors, flitting through the massive fireplace and dancing along the exposed beams of the canted fifteen-foot ceiling.

'So what do you think?' Sebastian asked, his hands deep in his pockets, shuffling from one foot to the other. The house was solid, it was warm and it felt more like a home than any place Romy had ever been. This place was him.

'It's just wonderful, Sebastian. I'm so happy you did not let it go.'

He gave her the grand tour. He showed her to her bedroom, which was located on the other side of the lounge room from the master bedroom where she assumed he would sleep. It was decorated in simple creams and caramels. Rustic. Masculine. Decorated by a man. By him alone. She felt strangely relieved that no female ghosts from his past had had a hand in creating the ambience of this so personal home.

She dumped her bag and sauntered back out to the lounge. Sebastian had created a fire but he was nowhere to be seen. She took a seat on the couch closest to the hearth.

A scrapbook of photos rested on a rustic old coffee-table. Romy picked it up to have a little flick whilst she waited but soon slowed as she realised it was a documentary of the history of the beach house. It showed photos of the Gibsons from when they were a young couple, through the hundreds of foster children who had come through their open doors.

She recognised Sebastian in several pictures: lifted high on bigger boys' shoulders after scoring what must have been the winning try in a match of touch football; arms folded, proud as punch as his foot rested carefully against a mammoth sandcastle; grinning, wrapped in the arms of Mrs Gibson in a 'family' portrait with a dozen other kids.

She heard the scuff of shoes on wood behind her as Sebastian came up with a couple of wine glasses.

'Oh, no, really, I couldn't—'

'It's cordial. Just looks nicer in these than in my mismatched old jam jars.'

She took the glass from him as he sat down beside her, careful not to brush her fingers against his. 'Thanks.'

The setting was so cosy. So quiet. So intimate. Romy felt as if they could chat about anything and she knew the walls would not talk.

'Sebastian, there has been one thought that has been bugging me for a while and I just have to come out and say it.'

'OK.' He leant back into the deep couch, and sipped on his drink.

'What if you can't have kids?'

'I can.'

She had expected a moment of considered thought. She felt the need to rephrase the question. 'I know you seem to be able to do everything you set out to do with hardly any effort, but this is something you sometimes cannot control. How do you really know you can?'

'Because Eleanor, my first fiancée, was pregnant.'

Romy could not have looked more surprised if he had thrown his cordial in her face.

'Sebastian,' she whispered. 'Was it…? Did she…? What…what happened?'

She shuffled around on the seat, pulling a leg beneath her as she had the night they had kissed in the car. This was her overture stance. She wanted information and she was not going to let go until she had what she wanted. And right then she wanted to know about the worst night of his life.

And he was going to tell her.

'We had not been getting along for some time. We hadn't gone as far as calling off the engagement but I was overseas, playing in one tournament after the other. I had just arrived home from overseas when I got the phone call from the hospital. It was late. I was jet-lagged. And I hadn't even known she was pregnant. She was bleeding and I had to be there. I got in the car and sped as fast as the car would take me. Just around the corner from the hospital I hit a patch of oil. I spun out of control and wrapped my car around a telegraph pole.'

Romy reached out and laid a hand over his. She wrapped her fine fingers around his and clasped on. He felt her strength seep through him and he went on.

'When I woke up I was in a hospital bed wrapped up to the neck in bandages and Eleanor was at my side. It was meant to be the other way around. I was meant to be comforting her.'

'She miscarried?' Romy asked, her voice thick.

Sebastian nodded.

'And your back. You were injured?'

He shrugged. 'I lived.'

'But you couldn't play professional golf any more.'

'Not without an injection and only risking further damage.'

She snuck closer and ran her hand across his shoulders. 'And we made you play today. Are you OK? Are you sore?'

She rubbed lightly across the back of his neck. He could not help but sit higher so her hand could rub across his stiff shoulder blades.

As though she understood his movement her fingers dug deeper, rubbing out the small constant ache and sending delicious shivers of another kind of warmth through his entire body. If he had been aching earlier he wasn't now.

He had to clear his throat before going on. 'I'm fine. I can play, but irregularly, and I've learnt how best to favour my injury.'

'I had no idea.'

'I'm glad. It's nice to know some things don't end up as a yellowed newspaper clipping at the bottom of a folder to be recalled every time your name is mentioned.'

He caught her blush, unnecessary though it was. That day in her conference room felt like a million years before. But it had been a crossroads for him. And he wouldn't change a second of his time since then. Good or bad. Because it had led to this point, with her at his side in his beach house, a place he only took those closest to him. With her running a smooth hand across his neck and looking at him as if she wanted to absorb every lick of pain he had ever experienced. And he had a feeling she could.

'I promise it still won't,' she said.

And he believed her. He believed every word she said. She was so open. So true. So honest.

About everything except about herself. If only he could get her to open up about her own feelings. Her own relationships. She had repressed her inner fire for so long and if he was to release it she could very well blame him for the torrent of irrepressible emotions that would no doubt follow.

He eased himself out of the couch. If he remained by her side in that warm room, that room so full of love and happy memories with her touching him like that, and looking at him like that, he might not be able to stop what could very well happen next.

And he doubted very much if she would respect him in the morning. And her respect was something he was finding himself clinging to more and more each day he knew her.

'It's late,' he said.

She sat where she was and just watched him, her big eyes round and compassionate.

'It's been a big day, and I think we could both do with a good night's sleep.'

She nodded and gave a great sniff. 'Sure.'

She unwrapped her legs from beneath her and rose from the chair. She had such grace it hurt to watch her ready to leave. She leaned towards him, the scent of her filling his nostrils, and she kissed him on the cheek. 'Goodnight, Sebastian,' she whispered against his cheek and he was undone.

He reached up and took her cheeks between his palms and turned her face to his.

He caught the shock in her eyes but it was so quickly followed by fervent acquiescence. A small groan escaped her lips before he crushed them to his own.

After his morning shower Sebastian searched the house for Romy but she was nowhere inside. He grabbed a duffle-coat and headed out the back door, across the rickety wooden path that meandered through sand-dunes covered in patches of rough grass until he reached the pristine white beach.

And there she was. Standing halfway between him and the water, her shoulders wrapped in a mohair blanket from the back of the couch, her cargo trousers rolled up to her knees, her feet bare. Her hair was swept back as the winter air whipped off the Pacific and flicked her low pony-tail in a fury at her back.

He paused. He had not seen her since the night before, when he had experienced the most astounding kiss of his life. A kiss that had spoken so much that they seemed unable to admit through words. A kiss that had ended all too soon with Romy pulling away in a wretched gasp and disappearing into her room and closing the door with a significant click.

She looked tired that morning and he knew she had slept as restlessly as he. With the knowledge they were a bare ten metres apart all night it had been achingly difficult.

'Grisham would love it here,' Romy said as Sebastian approached. 'And I don't know how you can drag yourself back to town after spending time here. It's heaven. If I were you I would never leave.'

'I'm often here on my own but the house craves company. I love it here most when Melinda and Tom and the kids come up for a couple of weeks. It's amazing, the house seems to blossom under their spirited attention.'

'Of course.'

Romy nodded and he guessed she was thinking it was he who craved the company not the house. But he was learning that it was all intertwined.

'Coming?' She motioned down the beach and took off at a slow ramble, expecting Sebastian to follow. How could he not? He was drawn to her. When she was around, that was where he wanted to be. And it hit him why it felt so different. It had nothing to do with loneliness and everything to do with her. So, freezing cold, barefoot and barely covered up in a duffle coat, he followed.

'So how about you and Antony? Do you plan to have kids?'

'Sebastian, don't ask about Antony, please.' Her feet now dug deep into the moist sand with every step.

'Come on, Romy. I thought I understood why you have not wanted to talk about him in the past but I've met the guy. I know he exists. And I could see by the look on his face that he is crazy about you. So stop pretending the guy isn't in your life and just tell me about him. I think you owe me at least that.'

Sebastian finished his speech, amazed he had managed to sound so nonchalant when his guts twisted along with every difficult word.

She shot him several looks from beneath her eyelashes as though weighing him up, checking he wasn't playing her. She had real trust issues, that one. Well, that was all the more reason for him to be a good friend and lend her his ear without recriminations about their two scintillating kisses, and without making her feel foolish. No matter what she said about the guy.

'Do you really want to know about Antony?'

More than you know, sweetheart. 'Sure. Spill the whole story. I bet it's one of the great romances.'

'It's just that I'm not used to talking about…' She waved her hand about as though the word she was looking for would spill from her fingertips. 'I talk about failed relationships all day, every day, and therefore don't want to jinx my own by airing it in the same way.'

Sebastian's heart slowly turned colder and colder. It was the only way he could do this. 'Well, look about you, Romy. No other lawyers, no coffee machines, no conference tables, even funny kidney-shaped ones. Just me, on a big empty beach with no memories.'

'Well,' she was still hesitant but he felt her confidence growing with each step, 'he's a lawyer. He lives in Boston half of the year.'

'I know all that, sweetheart. I don't want the guy's hat size. Just tell me about the two of you. Inspire me with the brilliance of your union. How did he propose? Did he write it in the sky?'

'No.' She laughed.

Good, he thought. *Relax, sweetheart, and tell me how a man managed to steal your so heavily guarded heart. And why you now seem on the verge of throwing all that away.*

'I…we were at a conference in Washington DC. He took me to dinner at a lovely little Georgetown bistro we both like. When the bill came, he paid.'

'And?'

'And we had always gone Dutch before. He's sensible like that. When I asked why, he said that there was no need to split expenses. His money would be my money from now on as he wanted nothing more than to make me his wife.'

That was a marriage proposal? This was a woman who deserved to be swept off her feet. She deserved to be lauded with praise and bombarded with daily truckloads of flowers. 'Not a real romantic, then?'

Romy frantically shook her head; several strands of hair had escaped their elastic confines and were caught on the ocean breeze. 'But romance is the last thing you need to make a relationship succeed. It blurs the lines so that any problems you may have can get lost in the fuzzy edges of the relationship.'

No! She couldn't really believe that, could she?

'Look at my parents. I don't think my father ever bought my mother a bunch of flowers or a box of chocolates in their life together, but they are the most devoted, in-sync couple I have ever known.'

Sebastian thought back on Romy's parents, the way her father grizzled at the obviously delicious dinner, the way her mother made sure he always ate well, the way they touched each other whenever they had the chance. Theirs was a marriage brimming with romance and Romy just couldn't see it. But now was not the time to tell her. Now was the time to get the dirt on her fiancé.

'So he proposed and then what?'

'And then I…'

If she said she broke down in tears and leapt onto Antony's lap, declaring her undying love, Sebastian thought he would have no choice but to throw himself into the freezing cold ocean, fully clothed.

'…asked him to give me a month to think about it.'

Sebastian stopped. His feet just refused to walk another step. So Jennifer had been right.

Romy must have felt he was no longer near her, as she too stopped a couple of metres away and slowly turned. Her hair whipped about her face, covering and uncovering her eyes so that Sebastian had no idea what was going on behind their hidden depths.

'The month is up,' she continued, no longer needing his encouragement. 'Antony is here, in Australia, to get my answer. And by tomorrow night he will have it.'

The question hung in the air between them. What would her answer be?

'How did *you* know?' she asked, bringing him back to earth and the roar of waves lapping at the nearby craggy rocks and the screech of hungry seagulls once more superseded his thoughts.

'Know what?'

'When you met the…women you wanted to marry?' A smile tugged at the corners of her mouth. Was that really Romy making a joke about marriage?

'I'm sure you've heard it all before.'

She shrugged. 'But I think I have to hear it from you.'

Romy watched the emotions play across Sebastian's face and she knew that no matter what else was going on in his mind, she was at the forefront of his thoughts.

Even above the whipping wind and the icy cold, the electricity between them was unmistakable. He had pushed and pushed and pushed until she had no choice but to tell him of the crossroads her life had reached. And now it was his turn. The final piece of the Sebastian puzzle would finally become known to her.

'Janet and I had known each other on and off for some years,' he began as he started walking again. Romy matched his slow pace. 'We always got along famously, had flirted madly for years though had never followed through on the promise, and after six months of marriage we knew why. It turned out we had a… misunderstanding. I misunderstood the level of her desire for a family and she misunderstood that my life was less about jet-setting charity golf tournaments and more about quiet weekends at the beach.'

Sebastian reached out and took Romy's arm to guide her around a precarious collection of driftwood hidden beneath deceptively soft piles of sand.

'And before that?' she asked, casually releasing her arm once they had passed the hazard.

'Sophie. My break-up with Eleanor coincided with the hoopla surrounding the end of my career, so I *relocated* to Europe, where I knew I would go unnoticed. Sophie was a waitress in a café I went to daily. She had no idea who I was, she was a kind ear and warm arms to sleep in at night. Being the gentleman it seems I have the misfortune of being, I asked her to marry me. We lasted a year in France, before Melinda had Delilah and I couldn't handle not seeing my niece and nephews grow up. I was wrong to bring Sophie here. She became dinner conversation for readers of the tabloid Press. Amazingly she lasted two years before she fled back home. And I don't blame her. We catch up on birthdays and at Christmas.'

They had reached the ragged rocks at the end of the thin beach. As one they turned and headed back towards the beach house.

'And Eleanor?'

'Eleanor was different.'

Romy glanced at Sebastian. So open. So vocal about his mistakes and his achievements both. And now he was silent. Romy gulped down the heartburn that had risen in her throat. 'How different?'

'Too much. Not enough. And then it was over.'

Eleanor was different all right, Romy thought. Eleanor was the one with whom he had been so close to starting the family he craved. Eleanor was the first one to provide him with a home after the Gibsons and could not live up to Sebastian's high expectations of what a family should entail. And since Eleanor he had tried again and again to get it right, only then with the added pressure of having to do so under the watchful eye of the tabloid Press.

No wonder he had been unable to forge a successful relationship since. She thought her friends at university and her mum's poker club had been a tough audience during her break-up with Liam, but the idea of going through that in such a public forum…

'Don't ask me, Romy. If you are looking for advice on whether to accept Antony's proposal I am the last one you should look to.'

How could she not look to him for answers? Her heart ached for him to fall to his knees in the sand, and tell her it was all a mistake, that only together could they forge on, irrespective of their past predicaments. Her knees tingled as she imagined him clutching at the blanket about her shoulders, drawing her down with him and showing her exactly how he felt in the most unforgettable manner imaginable.

'What should I say, Sebastian?' she asked, all but breathless. 'What should my answer be?'

He stopped and turned to her, his hands thrust deep into his coat pockets. The wind whipped his hair about his face; his cheeks were pink and dry from the ocean breeze.

'Why are you asking me?'

'Because we are...friends.' *Because the answer is yours to make and not mine. Because I cannot be responsible for destroying the delicate new balance you seem to have found in your life. Unless that is what you really want.*

'Friends?' His face was unreadable.

'Because I think if anybody has the answer it's you.' How could she make it more obvious? *Tell me, Sebastian.* She wished the thought from her head to his own.

He watched her closely and she sent him every telepathic message she could muster, but it was to no avail. 'I'm the last one who has the answer you're looking for, Romy.'

And then he turned and continued up the beach.

So that was it. He felt nothing for her. She had thrown herself at him, searching for something. Answers? Options? Proof that she had been so wrong all of these years? But she should have listened to her head. She should have known better. He had nothing to offer her. Romy's heart felt leaden beneath her ribs.

Sebastian dragged one leg after the other up the beach. What was she doing asking him, the guy she so vociferously claimed was the man least likely to know a thing about the subject, for marriage advice? Hadn't he proved he hadn't a clue? Then again, if he took her comments to heart, she was all but asking him to tell her to say no. And if she wanted to say no, and wanted him to agree…

He picked up the pace, knowing if she caught up to him and touched his sleeve with that soft, kitten-shy touch of hers that he would turn and drag her into his arms and beg her to say no.

But he was kidding himself. That was the last thing she needed. *He* was the last thing she needed. She had everything going for her. A great career, a great family, a stable fiancée. The woman was so sure of herself and her needs.

He had known Eleanor for several months, Sophie for a year and Janet forever before he had come to propose to them. Romy he had known for less than a week and the tumble of feelings she invoked in him were like nothing he had ever experienced. If he wasn't careful they could burn him up for good, leaving him with nothing to offer any other woman.

Sebastian reached the wooden steps leading to the beach house and took them two at a time. The lapping waves, the howling wind and the seagulls seemed far, far away. He had to get away from her and into a cold shower, and fast, because if he followed his screaming instincts it would be impossible to let her go.

And she was simply not his for the taking.

CHAPTER THIRTEEN

WHEN Romy came out after her shower a good hour later, Sebastian had put on a wonderful spread for lunch. Conversation had been polite, civilised. Romy had to do her best to act as though she was in one piece when she felt as though she was being kept together with failing sticky tape.

At the end of lunch Sebastian piled everything into a dishwasher, of course, turned to her and said, 'You've shown me yours, now I'll show you mine.'

'Excuse me?' she asked, suddenly fearing exactly how she had earned that third medallion in the golf game.

'My family.'

'Ah. I hardly think that's necessary.'

'You want to know as much about me as you can, do you not?'

How could he tell? Was she that transparent?

'So you can change me for the better?' he continued. 'I'm taking Melinda's kids to the zoo tomorrow. You can come with us.'

Romy nodded. Tomorrow. Tomorrow was Sunday. And by tomorrow night she planned to give Antony her answer. The opportunity to spend one more day in Sebastian's company was something she simply had to take. No matter how much it hurt to feel her heart being lost to him piece by piece, she could not deny herself one more day.

They had packed their bags, been driven back to Brisbane and were on a plane home before Romy knew it. Needing to make her own way home, at the gate Romy made up some ludicrous on-the-spot story about it being her regular cleaning of kitchen appliances day, and the fact he actually seemed to believe her left her a little worried. Sure, she liked to plan ahead…

Late the next morning she had rugged up in a pale angora sweater and beige woollen trousers and matching coat and had met Sebastian and his niece and nephews at the spectacular Melbourne Zoo. He had been awaiting her at the front gate dressed in a white T-shirt, black V-neck sweater and leather jacket. Justin had been right. Any given day the guy was a knockout but in leather he was breathtaking. Romy had been hard pressed to drag her eyes away when introduced to his three hyperactive cohorts.

She took to them straight away. They had Sebastian's cheek and boundless energy. The five of them did the rounds in record time. Monkeys and lions and tigers and more. And she was more than glad when they finally had the chance to sit and eat. If she thought a round of eighteen holes was tiring this was something else again. Walking the zoo with the three robust kids was positively exhausting but in such a heavenly way.

He is just so good with these kids, Romy thought as she watched Sebastian from over her lunch. He was rounding up Thomas, who had taken off after an unsuspecting peacock that had come too close looking for crumbs. *He would be an amazing dad and he knows it. And wants it. So how unbelievably unfair that he doesn't have it.*

Romy felt a twinge in her stomach as she realised that she would have to class herself as a part of the problem. A part of the mystifying conspiracy that was keeping this amazing guy away from his destiny. There was that word again, but she knew that for once in her life it fitted.

Since the moment he had walked into her office, asking for her help, she had never really taken his plight seriously. Perhaps because he never seemed to either, with his recipe for the perfect woman and his continuous flirtation. But how could she blame him? She had seen enough divorcees to know how much they were hurt. And humour was a perfectly reasonable defence mechanism.

And she had fallen for it all. She had believed the playboy image, she had believed his mask of frivolity and she had really not done one thing to help him in the way she should have.

This was a guy with enough money to spend his days travelling the world but who would rather be on call to babysit his nieces and nephews. This was a guy with enough money to support a dozen legal firms, who, despite most likely vehement advice, had never asked his wife to sign a pre-nuptial agreement.

And somehow in amongst this mess, despite her most vigorous efforts to disapprove of him, she had managed to see past the image and fall for the man. And that was her worst betrayal of all. By falling for him she must have sabotaged his ability to find someone else. She had been nothing but destructive and disobliging.

Well, the time for her procrastinating was over. The pieces of the Sebastian puzzle now fitted so there were no excuses. If she really loved him, she would go to the ends of the earth to make him happy.

'Sebastian,' she called out, trying harder than ever to keep the love from her voice. 'I have just had an epiphany.'

'An epify-what?' Thomas asked as he ran ahead of Sebastian to the table, not wanting to miss out on any of the leftover French fries.

'A great idea,' Chris explained, rolling his eyes at his hyperactive younger brother.

Sebastian winked at her before wiping a smudge of tomato sauce from Thomas's chin. 'What's your great idea?' He whipped Delilah onto his knee and grabbed her the bottle of juice her small arms could not reach.

'I am going to throw you a party.'

'A party! Yippee!' Thomas leapt onto the bench and flew to the ground, spinning about with the sort of energy only junk food could supply.

'You want to put on a party for me?' Sebastian asked, his expression suddenly wary.

'I do. It would be like Cinderella, but from Prince Charming's point of view.'

'Prince Charming, eh?' Sebastian puffed out his chest. 'I kind of like it.'

Delilah giggled over her juice.

'Hmm. I thought you would.'

'I thought finding me a wife was not a part of your job description.' Now, since her real epiphany, Romy thought she heard a thread of fear creeping into his voice. Uncertainty at least.

'It wasn't,' she said. 'But it seems to me time to change the rules. You certainly don't seem to be finding anyone on your own, even with all of my magnificent help, so I have to resort to this.'

'So it will basically be sort of like a cattle call. The women can parade before me, the suitor, and you, their judge and jury, and we can find me a woman!'

Thomas nodded along manically, before performing a very fine orang-utan impersonation. 'Me Tarzan. You Jane.'

'That's just about what I was thinking,' Sebastian laughed.

'Don't you take anything seriously?' Romy asked, desperate to bring him around to the idea. Her bag of tricks was empty. If he did not take to this plan she had nothing left.

'Like what?'

'Like money. Like marriage. Like...'

'Like you?'

Romy shrugged. 'Fine. Like me. I am making a very serious, and I think very brilliant suggestion here.'

Sebastian shook his head. 'Romy. Romy. Romy. I think I could safely say I take you more seriously than you do.'

'Hardly. I can't think of a subject I take more seriously. Having serious control of my life is so important to me.'

'Mmm. I've noticed.'

'So, since I am a serious woman, with a serious idea, will you seriously do as you're told?'

He looked so deep into her eyes as though searching for her motives in taking their plan to such a finite conclusion. Well, she had no intention of letting him win that sort of staring contest. His future happiness depended on it.

Finally he nodded. 'OK, then. You win. Prince Charming I will be. You can introduce me to a flock of applicable young women and this will finally all be over.'

But Romy felt as if she had not won at all.

That night Sebastian went alone to Janet's housewarming party bearing a gift of a gaudy

Egyptian statuette. It would have looked so ridiculous in his home but he knew she would adore it.

She met him at the door of her new apartment with a kiss to each cheek. She grabbed the gift and added it to a tableful in the hallway. 'I wasn't sure you would come,' she said, with a fair amount of guilt flushing her cheeks. 'I would have understood completely if you hadn't.'

'Yet here I am. Here to see you happily settled. And to see what my money bought!'

She slapped his arm playfully. 'You are a good man. Way too good for me.'

Janet dragged him out to the massive living room and introduced him to the room at large. A few people he knew, most he had never met, evidence of the quite separate lives that they had never managed to inhabit no matter how fond of one another they had been. Evidence of the fact that not only had Janet deceived him in convincing him they wanted the same things in life, but also that he had happily believed her. He understood they both had their reasons and so had taken his own advice and forgiven them both.

'So how did you get on with the luscious Ms Bridgeport?' Janet asked.

He narrowed his eyes and Janet chuckled.

'You rang me, darlin'! Asking for her number.'

'To secure her services as a lawyer, Janet.'

'Of course! Why else would a man like you want the phone number of a woman like her? I can remember the way the sparks fair flew off the two of you like you were a pair of flint stones. It was a show to be seen.'

Sebastian turned Janet to face him, all but having to click his fingers in front of her to garner her full attention. 'I promise you, Janet, I did not call her for a date the day after our divorce went through.'

Janet stared back, her hawk eyes looking deep into his own. 'I know that, sweetie. You would have called her with the best of intentions, to offer to help the crèche kiddies or volunteer for some charity doodad. But now, nearly a week after the fact, after having done the right thing by me, and by your own antiquated sense of fair play, what is the nature of your relationship with the spirited young lady?'

'She's most likely engaged,' he said, knowing that hardly answered the question.

'I didn't ask about her relationship with anyone else. Just about her relationship with you.'

'I…I really couldn't tell you, Janet.'

'Now, that's more like it.'

He could do nothing but stare.

'When I met her it took me two seconds to know the two of you would hit it off. So I signed on the dotted line without a second thought. Then I had to listen to her screwball views on the deadly gravity of marriage and stable foundations and continued optimism had just knew she was kidding herself. You are both as screwy and both as sure in your views of what a good marriage makes as one another and I figured by butting heads you would both be sure to shake a few of those notions loose. And it seems that I was right.'

She grabbed him by the hand and gave it a good squeeze. 'It seemed the least I could do after how shabbily I treated your kindness.' Apology over, she took a deep breath and her attention moved on. 'Now go forth and socialise.'

But if Sebastian wanted to socialise, if was with one person alone. As soon as the coast was clear he left. And in the car on the way home he pulled over to the side of the road and rang

Romy's number. His heart beat in his chest as the phone rang. And rang. And rang.

Romy'd had so much extra energy after her day with Sebastian's young buddies she'd felt as if she was bouncing off the walls, and so had taken an evening jog. Once home she leapt into the lift, which chugged and creaked its way to the top and she barely noticed.

As she opened the door the phone was ringing, and ringing and ringing. She decided to let the machine take it, but the caller hung up as soon as it clicked on.

Antony! She had all but forgotten what day it was. She stared at the phone as the machine buzzed and whirred as it reset itself. And she waited for it to ring again.

It rang and she leapt a good foot into the air. She rushed over and grabbed the cradle.

'Hello?'

'Hey, Romy.' The voice was so familiar. She relaxed a very little.

'Hey, Antony. How was your weekend? Did you get everything done you had to?'

'Sooner than expected. So I do apologise for forcing you to go away on the golf trip. Though I knew it would be great for you career, I only wish I hadn't forced you to babysit that schmuck, Sebastian Fox.'

Romy clutched so hard on to the phone she had instant pins and needles in her fingers.

'He's not a schmuck, Antony. In fact, he is far from it.'

'Come on, Romy. Standing up for your client in a public forum is one thing but you have to admit this guy is a flake.'

'I will admit no such thing.'

'It's OK. We all have to kiss clients' butts at some stage in our career. I understand.'

'That's not it at all.'

'So what is it, then?'

Romy took a breath to calm herself. It had not been her intention to fight with Antony over Sebastian. She had never had cause to raise her voice with him before. They'd had such a placid relationship. This was the most challenging of her he had ever been.

'I'm just saying you have been misinformed, OK?'

'OK. Fine.'

She waited for more. But that was it. Challenge over. Did the guy have no backbone? No gumption? Maybe. But wasn't that exactly the reason she had gravitated towards him in the first place?

'So let's move on,' he said, his voice dry. 'I think you know why I really called. Or do you not wish to discuss this over the phone? Perhaps you would prefer we do this over dinner. Somewhere suitably romantic.'

He could not have said the word 'romantic' with any less enthusiasm. And Romy felt the ground beneath her drop away as she realised that, though this was what she thought she'd always wanted, if she had to live a lifetime with a man like that she would waste away into a quiet little mouse within no time. And no matter what other facets of her personality she had competing to be the primary Romy on any given day, none of them would bear to defer to timid Romy!

'Come on over, Antony. I'll put on dinner here.'

'Fine. I'll see you in an hour.'

He rang off then Romy took the phone off the hook. Tonight was not to be a night of interruptions.

Sebastian had hung up as soon as Romy's machine kicked in. His was not a message she should hear from a machine.

He turned the car around and drove to her place. He buzzed the apartment and nobody answered.

He tried calling several more times throughout the night but she still wasn't home. Or she wasn't answering. It was Sunday night. The end of the month. What if Antony was there to get his answer? The longer the night went on the more disheartened Sebastian became until later that night when he switched off his bedside lamp he felt more disconsolate than he remembered feeling in his whole life.

It was after eleven and Romy was exhausted, but after spending the last two hours with Antony she felt in great need of being enveloped in a pair of loving arms.

She knocked on her parents' door. She knew they would be up—they were both night owls, another thing they had in common to make them so perfect for one another. She heard mad scrambling of dog claws on the tiles and the clack of her mother's sandals behind them.

'Romy! What a nice surprise. We finished dinner hours ago, and it was only a casserole. Would you like me to reheat you some?'

Romy stepped inside and hugged her mum with one arm while holding Grisham at bay with the other. 'No, thanks, Mum. I ate already.'

'Come in. Come in. Your father's in the den watching the late news. Why don't you go join him and I'll bring you some sweets?'

'Actually I wanted to talk to you.'

'Oh.' Her mother stopped flurrying to look her daughter in the eye. 'OK. In the kitchen? I'm halfway through making a batch of ginger snaps for the poker-trip fundraiser.'

'Sure, the kitchen's fine.'

Romy trudged after her mother, rubbing Grisham behind the ear the whole way, but once they reached the end of the hall he branched off and rejoined Romy's father in the den, turning and turning and turning on the mat until he had the perfect position at his master's feet.

'Hey, Dad.'

'Hey, honey. Mum didn't tell me you were coming over—'

'It's all right, Dad, stay there. I'm going to help Mum with her cookies. I'll come join you in a bit.'

'Ginger snaps?' he asked.

'That's the rumour.'

'Sneak me one when they're done, OK?'

'I promise.' Romy moved through to the kitchen, shutting the door behind her.

Her mother looked up from the kitchen bench. 'It's a behind-closed-doors sort of talk, then, is it? What's up?'

'I turned Antony down tonight.'

'Aah. The American who proposed a while back?'

'Yep.'

'Good.'

Romy glanced up at her mother, feeling a twinge of anger at the easy dismissal when for her the decision had seemed so hard. 'You never even met him; why would you say that?'

'Because if it took you a month to decide—heck, if it took you a day to decide—then he was not the one for you. And as you say your father and I never even met him. Yet compare him to that other friend of yours, Sebastian; you sure brought him over to meet us quick smart.'

'This has nothing to do with Sebastian,' Romy said.

Cynthia rolled the cookie ingredients into palm-sized balls and laid them on greased paper. 'Doesn't it?'

'No. Yes. Maybe.' Romy sank her face into her hands. 'That's the thing, Mum; for years I would have thought Antony was exactly the kind of guy for me. He was quiet, patient, upstanding—'

'Sounds more like the recipe for a good priest than a good husband.'

'But don't you see, for so long I have known exactly what I wanted and I have touted it to every one of my clients, knowing it to be a truth? I just always wanted a peaceful, perfect marriage like you and Dad always had.'

'Peaceful?' Her mother almost choked on her laughter as she carried the tray to the hot oven. 'Perfect? You think we had it perfect?'

'Well, OK, not perfect. But you were always so obviously in love. You never fought. And you made me feel so secure.'

Cynthia closed the oven and set the timer. She then grabbed the mixing bowl, which still held the remnants of the biscuit mix, and plonked it in front of Romy as she always had when she was a kid.

'OK. Let's take a couple of steps back. I am so very glad to hear that we always made you feel secure, darling, as that was our prime focus. To let you know that we loved you always. But we fought.'

'But I never saw you—'

'Exactly, you never saw us. We fought like cat and dog, your father and I, but never in front of you if we could at all help it.'

'Wow.'

Cynthia tucked her daughter's hair behind her ear. 'Once, when you were little, I even moved out of home for about a month.'

Romy sat up straight, a fingertip covered in ginger snap mix stopped halfway to her mouth. 'You what?'

'We had had a whopper, about something so silly I can't even remember what it was, and I walked out. I packed a bag, full of my best clothes but no underwear—we still laugh at that one—and I moved in with your aunt. I came back home every day while your father was at work to be with you, but as soon as he was in the front door I was out the back. It took for me to come back to your aunt's one night to find she had repacked my bag, made me a casserole to take home for my family and kicked me out.'

'I don't remember a second of it.'

'You were too little to remember, thank goodness. But it goes to show that just because you did not see the struggles, doesn't mean they didn't happen.'

'My whole life I have wanted a marriage like yours.'

'That is not such a bad thing. Your dad and I do have one of the good ones.'

'But to me that meant a serious, deferential sort of love.'

Cynthia shook her head and smiled. 'God help the man who would expect you to be deferential, my sweet girl.'

Romy's thoughts swung directly to Antony. That was exactly what he had seemed to expect. Above and beyond all of his good qualities he wanted her to be as quiet and patient and upstanding as him, and in her heart of hearts she had known that wasn't her.

And then there was Sebastian. He baited her every chance he had as he seemed to thrive on her being continually on the verge of slapping him. He encouraged that wild and wilful side of her she had always thought she would need to suppress in order to impress a good man.

'So, my darling, go out into the world with the new knowledge that without conflict there is no passion. Without the fights there is no making up. A healthy relationship should not be only about mutual respect and a shared dream for the future but must also be about passion and delight and newness. A healthy relationship will grow and surprise forever. Marriage is deadly serious but without a good dash of silliness you will be bored out of your mind in a week!'

Romy ran a finger around the remains of the bowl.

'But I think you already knew all of that or you wouldn't have made such a smart decision today.'

'Why does she get to eat the cookie mix?' Romy's father asked from the doorway.

'Because she did a good thing today,' Cynthia said, tucking her hand beneath Romy's chin to make sure she understood. Romy nodded and smiled.

'What did she do that was so great?' her father asked, coming up behind her mother and trying to get to the oven. 'Did she refill the windscreen-wiper water on your car? Did she order a new gas cylinder? Did she pick up a bottle of milk on the way home?'

'No. She did not.'

'So?' he asked, his voice reaching bellow levels.

'So, that's why she did not get the ball of cookie dough waiting for you on the kitchen bench.'

George leapt to the kitchen bench with the agility of a man twenty years younger and ten kilos lighter. 'Is this for me?'

'That is for you, my love.'

He took the plate, carrying it as if it held the world's most precious cargo. He walked over to the table, gave his wife a light kiss on the top of the head then without another word went back to his den.

And then Romy knew. It had been in front of her all that time but she had built such a wall of sense and reason in front of her eyes she had not seen it.

Romance was not just flowers and chocolates. It was not just paying for dinner nor was it only skywriting your love. It was all those things but it was so much more.

Romance was cooking for your husband. It was making a fuss over how much you loved your wife's cookies. It was giving up your window seat on a plane. Romance was every little thing you could do to show someone you loved them.

And Romy knew that there was no better way to be true to her love for Sebastian than to make all of his dreams come true. She would do all she had to do to help him find the mother of his children. If she had to let him go to do that, then it would be the most romantic thing she had done in her life.

CHAPTER FOURTEEN

'HONEY buns is here,' Gloria hissed as Romy walked into work on Monday morning.

Romy skidded to a halt, skimming an alarmed glance at her office door.

'But don't panic, he's not in there. He went down to the real-estate guys. He's selling his house.'

Romy blanched. He couldn't be! Unless... 'Did he say if it was his beach house or the big house here?'

Gloria held up a wait-a-minute finger as she answered the phone. She nodded and said a lot of 'yep's before hanging up. 'Honey buns is on his way back, so you can ask him yourself.'

Romy flicked a glance over her shoulder. The coast was clear. 'Look, I have to see Libby Gold, at her home, right now.'

Sebastian knew the month was up. He knew her decision would have been made but she did not know how to break it to him. It was not as though it would affect him one way or the other, but she couldn't bring herself to rehash the conversation and its subsequent outcome. It had been hard enough avoiding the subject with Gloria all morning.

'What should I tell him?' Gloria yelled at her retreating back.

'Tell him I will be with another client all…week and tell him I will keep him updated on the party plans and that I will see him Saturday night.'

And Romy took off at lightning speed, calling Libby on the way to even check that she was free. Libby met Romy at the front door of her beautiful Toorak mansion with a flurry of tears and a bone-crushing hug.

'Libby! Is everything OK?'

'Everything's perfect,' she said between sobs. She beckoned Romy into her plush home, sat her down on a feather-soft couch and called for drinks and nibbles. She shot a look over her shoulder and whispered, 'Jeffrey has moved back home.'

'He has? For good?'

'For now,' Libby said, her voice stronger than Romy had ever heard it. 'I took him out to dinner as you suggested and told him how I felt, what I wanted, how it would have to be if he decided to come home. I gave him one last chance and without hesitation he took it.'

Romy gave her deliriously happy client another great hug. 'Oh, Libby, I am so happy for you. I really am.'

'But what about your record?' Libby asked as a flash of the timid woman of a week before shone through the new and improved veneer. 'You can no longer say not one of your clients has reconciled with their spouse.'

Romy shook her head. 'Forget about it, Libby. Maybe you can be the beginning of a new record. Perhaps I will become the matchmaking lawyer. The one to turn to when you hit a bump in the road and need a little legal advice and support to get you over your hurdle.'

'That would be much nicer,' Libby said. 'Now, what about you and your young man?'

'Oh. No, Libby. He's another client, that's all.'

Libby grinned. 'Who's another client?'

Romy snapped her runaway mouth shut.

'So, has our lovely young divorce lawyer finally found the one to bring her over to the other side? Have you too been given one last chance?'

One last chance?

The whole week with Sebastian had made her feel as if she was experiencing so many things for the last time. She had lapped up the opportunity to feel her heart beat so hard against her chest it became difficult to breathe, to take a walk along the beach with a man who made her stretch her imagination and capacity to forgive, to kiss with such potency she all but lost herself in the sensation.

But it was ridiculous. Why should she be doing anything for the last time? Sebastian was an example to her. An example that she should never give up hope, never stop looking for that which would fulfill her, never disallow the chance to overreach and even possibly fail, as there was always another chance just around the corner. All it took was forgiveness. And not forgiveness of those who might have hurt you or disappointed you but forgiveness of yourself. Forgive, gather the pieces, and start afresh with the very same capacity for hope and excitement with which you began.

'I have been given more than that, Libby. I have been given a lifetime of last chances,' Romy said, and Libby looked as confused as she ought. 'Now back to you. Tell me all about your dinner. I want to hear every last magnificent detail.'

By Friday afternoon Romy felt as though her life had been turned inside-out, wrung out and unfolded until she was fresh and new again.

Her mind brimming with ideas, Romy had another epiphany. The idea had been brewing since her conversation with Bridget on the way to Sanctuary Cove, when it occurred to her that though she had come up with numerous programmes to help the adults involved with divorce she had not yet done anything for their children.

And with her thoughts never far from Sebastian it came to her one night that he would be perfect to run a sporting camp, through the firm, for underprivileged kids and kids from broken homes. Via Gloria he had leapt at the idea and sent back a promise not only to run it as a fully fledged foundation, but also to fund the programme himself.

So, holed up in her office, closed off to all phone calls and further messages from *anyone*, even—and especially—her top clients, Romy had set to organising the legal side of the foundation regarding money, naming rights, insurance, location and all sorts of other bits and pieces so that too would be ready for a big announcement on Saturday night.

The party, which the firm had touted as little more than a welcome bash for their big new client, had taken on a life of its own and anyone and everyone from Melbourne society was going to be there.

'It's going to be a beautiful party,' Gloria sighed as they packed up the office. 'I'm thinking I'll need a new dress.'

'Hmm. I'm picturing long and black?'

'Well, that's where you're wrong.'

'I am?' Romy tried to picture Gloria in anything but black but couldn't do it.

'Yes. It's going to be short!' Gloria huffed, her nose high in the air. 'How about you? Do you have a dress? Or maybe even a date?'

Gloria knew exactly what she was asking. Would Antony be her date? 'Are you asking for a lift, Gloria?'

'Sure. Why not? Unless, of course, I would be getting in the way.'

'Not at all,' Romy said. 'I'll get the cab to pick you up on the way.'

Gloria shot her a bemused smile. 'Excellent. A trip to the Ivy in a cab. *Très* glamorous.'

Glamorous. Elegant. The party of the season. *It will be nothing less than perfect,* Romy thought. She only hoped that it worked and that Sebastian could find what he really wanted.

Sebastian entered the ballroom of the Ivy Hotel, glanced around the swelling room, and recognised many of the luminaries and Melbourne socialites happy to be out of the house on a chilly winter's night. But there was only one person he wished to see. One person he had spent a week trying to speak to face to face who he knew had spent a week avoiding him.

In that week he'd tried to slip back into his old routine of planning with his manager, deciding upon which celebrity golf matches to play, which charities to endorse, catching up on his investment portfolio. He had managed to feel involved for a day before admitting they had not held the same interest they had a week before. Before he had met her.

And then Gloria had contacted him with Romy's idea for the sporting camps and it was as if a light had switched on in his mind. It was perfect. He could teach golf and other sports to underprivileged kids, he could use his fortune in a way that would fulfill him in a way simply making the money never had, and he could honour his foster parents for giving him the opportunities they had. In a week she had managed to create the foundation from the ground up. She surprised him again and again, even *in absentia*.

And then he saw her. She stood at the bar with her back to him but he knew it was her. He knew her slender curves, which were set off by her gorgeous backless dress, a snug length of embroidered golden silk. He knew the timbre of her hair, which was swept back into an elegant chignon, and held in place by a large, intricate barrette. He knew the shape of her slim ankles above the impossibly high, spindly shoes.

And then just before he reached her, just as he was about to trust his voice had the strength to call out her name, he stopped short, his gaze drawn to her lower back, where the unbelievably sexy backless dress ended in a flirtatious V, revealing a playful butterfly tattoo, the size of a dollar coin.

The butterfly. The symbol of chaos. The tattoo that she had acquired as a sixteen-year-old was a tribute to her rebellious, passionate side that she so wished to obscure. But even with her fixation on crystals, suspicions and good-luck charms, even with her almost fanatical addiction to planning each and every minute of her day, her week, her life, she had never had it removed. And for some reason that night she had it on show.

As though she had sensed him arrive at her back, she turned. Large disc earrings clinked and glittered, drawing Sebastian's halted gaze back to her face.

He had never seen her look more beautiful. Her lips were moist, her eyes were striking and her countenance was all the more savoured for their parting.

'Hello, Sebastian,' she said, but it might as well have been *take me here and now* for the sensation it aroused through the length and breadth of him.

'Evening, Romy. How long have you been here?'

'Not long. How about you?'

'Not long.' The hairs on the back of his neck stood on end and he knew why. He was waiting for someone to appear at Romy's side and whip him away from this little island of happiness. He couldn't stand it. He had to know. 'Are you here…alone?'

'Your drink, ma'am,' the barman called out to Romy. She turned quickly to take her drink and Sebastian thought he saw her hands shaking. So he wasn't the only one feeling a little overwhelmed by their proximity. Maybe it was the occasion, maybe she'd had too many drinks already, but he didn't think so. She was as nervous about seeing him again as he was her.

'Shall we do the rounds?' she asked, either forgetting his question or ignoring it. Either way he took a step away from the bar and followed.

Romy kept a step ahead of Sebastian as much as she could the next half an hour. She had no choice. She couldn't bear watching him walk before her, his magnificent form confined in a beautifully cut dinner suit, his hair slicked back into a most debonair style, his faint intoxicating scent of soap a pursuing shadow. He looked so gorgeous she had almost melted into a quivering mess when he'd approached her at the bar.

To keep her mind and hands busy, she introduced him to her friends and colleagues alike and finally, once the rest of the room was exhausted, she introduced him to Samantha.

If anyone there that night could provide a wonderful, loving home for Sebastian, it would be her. Sweet, pretty, lovely Samantha ran the crèche at her office. After starting the conversation off, Romy left them to their own devices and, feeling in dire need of a shoulder to lean on, she caught up with Alan.

'How has life been treating you, Romy?' Alan asked.

'Just fine, thanks, Alan. And you? How are the wife and kids?'

'Divine and unruly respectively.'

'How did you two meet again?' she asked, watching the first steps of what she had planned to be a budding romance. The idea ate her up inside and she had to keep repeating the silent mantra, *it is best for him, it is best for him.*

'My last year at university. She worked as a merchandiser in the campus supermarket whilst studying fashion at college. She was stacking soup cans into a pyramid and—'

'And you knocked the whole thing over with your shopping trolley, right?'

'No, some hunky human-movements major did that. One stray can rolled two aisles away, where I stood on it and went for a six. Broke my collar-bone.'

'That's right! You came to graduation in a neck brace, didn't you?'

'Mmm. But I also came to graduation with a girlfriend on my arm.'

'That's so sweet, Alan, really. And you're still, you know, happy?'

'Happier than ever. There's no rhyme or reason to how these things work, Romy. Every couple in the world has an original tale to tell.'

'And they survive or fail on their own specific merits or mistakes, nevertheless,' Romy finished.

'That they do. So what's with all the philosophising, my friend? You practising a new closing statement?'

Romy cleared her vision. 'Mmm. Something like that.'

'Must be a big project; we all missed you at Fables Wednesday night.'

'It's been a big week. Organising the party, creating the foundation, catching up on casework I did not have time for the week before.'

'Quite took you over, didn't he?'

'Sorry?'

'Our young Mr Fox. He seems to have appropriated an inordinate amount of your time. I hope it's been worth it.'

More than he'll ever know, Romy thought, but she felt she needed to get off the subject and quickly.

'*Young* Mr Fox! Please, Alan! He's older than you!'

'I know. But I kind of have a soft spot for him, you know.'

'Because with him as your partner you always won the company golf games, I suppose,' she joked, keeping a very close eye on young Mr Fox, who was still happily chatting away with Samantha on the other side of the dance floor.

'Not at all. Being an old married man, I always felt like an older brother. He's a good guy with a run of bad luck in the female stakes and that's how he gets judged by the world.'

'I think you're right there.' Romy flinched as Sebastian put an arm around Samantha's waist and drew her out to the dance floor.

'But somehow I think that bad luck might have come to an end,' Alan said.

Romy thought he was probably right. The smile had not left Sebastian's face since he had met Samantha and she had done just as Romy expected and blossomed under Sebastian's attention. But she would. She was a lovely woman. Great with kids. She was funny, she was kind, she was perfect for him. She just had to be.

Romy turned to smile at Alan, expecting him to be admiring the couple on the dance floor too, but he was staring at her with a big sappy smile on his face.

'What?'

'Nothing.' He shook his head.

'What? What are you smirking about, you big goof? Did I miss something?'

'You bet you did, but I think I can rectify that.'

As Sebastian and Samantha slow-danced their way Alan grabbed Romy's hand and twirled her out onto the dance floor.

'Whoa, Fred Astaire! Where did you learn a move like that?'

'Well, Ginger, my wife learned pretty quick smart that I had no sense of innate grace so figured it would take some learnin'.'

'You learned good.'

Alan continued to sweep Romy across the floor, twirling and dipping and leading until she was almost out of breath. When the music stopped, Romy was glad for the moment to catch her breath.

'Hey, Fred,' she called to her partner when the music started again but he was gone, dancing off into the distance with a laughing Samantha.

So that left Romy in the middle of the floor without a dance partner. And in the same boat as…

CHAPTER FIFTEEN

'SEBASTIAN,' she whispered as his arm stole around her bare back, his sure fingers splaying low and firm and drawing her into his arms with such surety you would have thought they had cut such a move a thousand times before.

'Shall we?' he asked, his beautiful grey-green eyes insisting *no* was not an option.

No was not an option for her either. Not for a second. The feeling of being in his arms over-rode every altruistic notion she'd had in setting up this evening.

'We shall,' she said, feeling like Cinderella being swept up in the arms of Prince Charming and with the same sense of foreboding that once the dance was over…

Sebastian caught the beat of the lilting song and swept her across the floor. If she thought Alan had been a good dancer, Sebastian made him seem like a donkey with four left feet. The natural athlete he was, Sebastian had so much innate grace.

'I thought you had a back injury,' she said. 'I seem to remember mention of it in a list you once gave me.'

'Mmm. Funny, though, I can't feel a lick of pain right now.'

His hand reached an inch lower until it brushed the V where her dress began below the line of her hip. His finger lightly traced the outline of her small tattoo. She could feel the planes of his fingertip run over the slightly roughened spot, and the delicate touch was so erotic her knees almost buckled beneath her.

But rather than shift his hand to a more modest position, she sank into him, drinking in his familiar scent. She closed her eyes, let go of all of her natural instincts to lead, to control, and simply followed. As she would happily follow him to the ends of the earth if that was what would make him happy. If only.

'I heard a rumour that you were selling your house,' she asked. She risked a look and saw him smile with such sweetness she knew he understood her instantly.

'Not the beach house,' he said.

'That's a relief! But why sell your house here?'

'I took some good advice from a friend. The house was bought especially to house a large family. But I've since learned it's all about love, marriage, *then* the baby carriage.'

Romy leaned her forehead against his shoulder, unable to look him in the eye any longer. She would only give herself away if he kept talking like that. 'Have you got somewhere else in mind?'

'I've moved in already. It's a two-bedroomed place near Melinda and Tom's. A place for me. With room for maybe one other. If it comes to that.'

That was a huge step for him. He was so ready to move on and it made her feel so proud. And yet so sad. It only proved that after that night she would have nothing further to offer him.

'My turn for a question,' Sebastian said.

She opened her eyes on a sigh. 'Yes?'

'Why didn't you bring Antony tonight? You have worked so hard and you look so beautiful, it seems a waste not to share a night such as this with him.'

He had to know some time, and better to clear the air between them completely. 'Antony is in Boston.'

'Already?'

Romy could feel his hand clench down on hers and she understood his anger. 'Sebastian, Antony is home in Boston because I said *no*.'

He came to such a complete stop Romy was glad he had a tight hold of her or the inertia would have flung her out into the crowd. 'So you and Antony…'

Romy ached for the heady sense of freedom she had felt in his arms and she panicked, feeling the song nearing its end. Why would the fates allow her this all too brief taste of what she so desired before she had to give it up? Three and a half minutes did not seem too much to ask against a lifetime without him. She rocked back and forth, hoping he would get the hint.

'Antony and I are not engaged. We are not dating. We are nothing. OK? Now, shut up and dance with me.'

But Sebastian had other ideas. He took her hand and led her outside to the balcony, where ivy climbed the rustic brick walls and numerous potted gardenias delivered a heady scent on the night breeze.

'Sebastian. What are we doing here? Your guests…'

'They are not my guests, Romy. I hardly know a soul in there.'

Romy gasped, lifting a hand to cover her flushed throat. 'How thoughtless of me. I should have invited your sister, shouldn't I? God, and I tried so hard to make it perfect. I couldn't even get the guest list right.'

'Romy! Stop it.'

'OK.' But her glance kept stealing inside as though she was missing out by being outside, alone with him. This was not at all what he had expected. Or what he wanted.

'Romy. Tonight I am going to announce to the world the name of the woman I am planning to marry.' That was not the way he had planned to broach the subject with her but at least it got her attention.

Her gaze skittered back to him, her eyes wide with shock. 'You are?' Her voice was weak as a kitten's meow.

'I am. I was thinking maybe you could help me.'

She swallowed and her body felt rigid in his arms. 'I can?'

He grabbed a hold of her arms as she began to sway. By the sound of her repetitive questions she had switched to autopilot. This was not the way. This was not the time. He had to get her back on to manual drive or the time would never present itself.

'You can,' he said. 'Let the band know, during their next break, that I will take the stage. I'm sure they won't mind my using their mike to make my announcement.'

'You are going to do it on stage? In front of everybody? You are that certain of your choice?'

He looked deep into her eyes, willing her to catch up with the conversation at hand. 'I am that certain.'

'OK.' She finally seemed to gather her wits. She pulled away, taking a couple of steps back. 'Don't you worry about a thing. I will organise the lot.'

'Thanks, Romy.'

'No worries. And Sebastian.'

He held his breath.

'I am really so very happy for you.'

And then she walked away.

Romy did as Sebastian had asked. She cued the band, she alerted the lighting guys and even made sure the whole crowd would have champagne at hand when the announcement was made.

For the fifteen minutes it took, her body shook involuntarily and her legs threatened to collapse. So once everything was in place, and before she turned into a blithering pumpkin before everyone's eyes, she took off.

There were so many cabs outside she leapt into the first at hand. She still had the sense of mind to tip the driver and thank him before she leapt from the car and tore into her apartment building.

And only once inside did the tears threaten to spill. Tears of exhaustion, tears of bereavement.

Romy ran inside but her shift dress was so tight she could only shuffle. There was no way she would make it up the stairs without tearing massive slits in the side of her dress. But the damn dress had cost her a week's wages and, for a girl paying a mortgage and a luxury-car loan, ruining it was out of the question. She reached the lift, and banged the button again and again and again.

'Damn you, lift!' she screamed out as the rickety old contraption jerked and mumbled its way from the floor above. Finally it reached the ground and Romy tore at the doors, opening the grate with all the strength she could manage. When inside she reached to drag the cage closed but an arm reached out and stopped her.

'Sebastian! What on earth are you doing here?'

'What am I doing here?' he asked, his voice ragged. 'What are *you* doing here? Why didn't you stick around?'

'I...felt sick.' That was the truth. She felt as though she wanted to purge all of the heartache that clenched at her stomach. 'I guess I missed your big announcement.'

'Actually you didn't. I saw you run off and there was no way I could make my announcement without you there. You were such a major player in the decision I could hardly go ahead with you not there.'

'Sorry.'

'Don't sweat it,' he said. 'I'd always wanted to say "follow that car" and tonight I got my chance.'

The lift began to ping and buzz and make all sorts of upset noises, as the grate had been open too long. Sebastian hesitated before leaping in and closing the door.

'I spoilt everything,' Romy admitted, her voice a harsh whisper.

'Not at all,' he promised. 'In fact, without you—'

The old lift suddenly creaked, louder than Romy had ever heard it creak before, then shuddered to a grinding halt between floors.

'God, why?' Romy threw her arms out in defeat. 'Why now, you stupid old stupid lift?'

'So much for being solid and dependable,' Sebastian said with a smile.

'Let's just say I've discovered of late that solid and dependable are not two qualities I should have rated so highly,' Romy said, giving the cage a good, hearty kick that damaged her new shoes, which upset her even more than the uncompromising lift.

'You don't know how glad I am to hear that.'

Sebastian suddenly seemed closer. He was definitely in her personal space and getting closer.

'Why are you glad?' she asked, her mind reeling with the possible reasons.

'Because it means that you are finally over your ridiculous fixation with good boys and may just be ready to take me on.'

Her breathing grew instantly laboured. Dared she hope he really meant what he was saying?

'You want me to take you on?'

'Why not?' His eyes glittered with mischief. 'You're easy on the eye, able to string a sentence together, you reach my chin when not in heels. You see, my old back injury means I cannot bend my neck for prolonged periods of time—'

'And I am employed. I get it. Though since you came along I have not been able to win a divorce case. I even sent my one and only remaining client back to her husband! I don't know how much longer I will be employed if I keep that up.'

'You could always run the Gibson Foundation with me,' he said, his voice low and tempting and showing that he had other things on his mind than his new project.

Romy held out her hands against his chest, halting his travels her way. She fought to disengage from the feeling of the most heavenly chest muscles curved against her palms.

'Sebastian, you are only just divorced, I have even more recently turned down a very real proposal of marriage. Apart from the timing being terrible, I think the worst thing for either of us would be to turn to each other as interim company.'

She knew as she said it what a liar she had made of herself. And the look on Sebastian's face was so indulgent she wondered if he thought the same.

'Who said anything about interim company?'

Romy swallowed down the dangerous wave of hope rising through her body.

'And as to this being bad for *us*,' he said, 'that is the most ridiculous thing you have ever said! Our timing could not be more perfect. Without our mix of mistakes and misunderstandings we would not be at the exact point where we are now. We might always have been as overwhelmingly attracted to one another as we are, but under these precise circumstances we have had to take our time, to talk, to get to know one another, and ourselves. And now…'

'And now?' Romy asked, her heartbeat rising to a happy crescendo as it seemed Sebastian was about to tell her the words she so desperately wanted to think were true.

He took a step forward, now so close their arduous breath intermingled.

'And now…'

He leaned the last precious centimetres until their lips touched and Romy's spirit soared. She savoured his sweet taste, revelling in not only his kiss but also his nearness, the fact that she had dreamt of this moment over and over during her heavy sleeps of the last week. But all too soon she had to pull away. First she had to know.

'What about Samantha?'

'Who?' Sebastian asked, his mind addled by her sweet soft flavour. When he realised she was serious his mind ticked over any of his exes who might for some ridiculous reason have her worried about her position.

'Samantha. I introduced her to you tonight. You danced with her.'

'Sure.' He nodded along blindly. 'Samantha. What about her?'

'Did you…I mean, did you like her?'

He took Romy by the shoulders, having to stop himself from shaking the nonsense from her tripping tongue.

'Of course I liked her. But I have no idea what you are trying to say.'

'Tonight,' she whispered, her body all but quaking in his arms as the fight left her. 'I set this whole night up for you to meet her. And if not her, somebody. Not just anybody, but the one. The one who would make you happy.'

But didn't she realise that was who he had in his arms right that second?

'You were hoping I would fall in love with the woman of my dreams tonight?'

'Yes,' she said, but her voice wavered and tears gathered at the corners of her big, sad, blue eyes.

'But don't you see it was too late for that?'

She shook her head. 'No! It's never too late I know that now.'

'So what am I doing here, with you, trapped in this ridiculous old lift instead of doing the rounds with the many and varied, delightful women you had laid out for me at the party?'

'I don't know.'

'You don't?'

She shook her head but he thought he saw a spark, the slightest glimmer of hope that maybe she did know but was simply not willing to believe. And, considering even getting to that point had taken some serious revision of her long-entrenched views on relationships, he was not surprised. It seemed there was no use in telling her, as her mind was a tumble of deals and promises and hopes and dreams, and he was certain there was still a hint of doubt. He would simply have to show her how he felt.

He gathered her in his arms, leaning her back against the flat surface of the lift wall, and kissed her. And this was not just any kiss. This was the kiss of a man who knew what he wanted. It was the kiss of a man who held on to the woman of his dreams. It was the kiss of a man who had realised he finally had what he always knew he always wanted.

When he pulled away, several long moments later, Romy's tears and shakes were gone. In their place was a woman who knew exactly what was going on.

'You're here for me,' she said, her voice bolstered by comprehension.

He nodded. 'I am here for you.'

'Because I am the one you want.'

'Because you are the one I want.'

'Because you…' She finally lost her nerve.

'Because I, Sebastian Fox, yearning romantic, love you, Romy Bridgeport, soft-headed rationalist.'

'Oh, Sebastian. Are you sure? I mean, do you really?'

He took her face in between his palms and promised, 'More than I thought I had the capacity to love anyone.'

'I love you too. I love you. I love you,' she yelled, in a rush of liberated emotion. She threw herself into his arms so hard he rocked back against the other side of the rickety lift and fought to keep his footing as the box swung back and forth on its rusty old cables.

'Hey, sweetheart, be careful there; I don't know how much excitement this old lift can take.'

'I don't care,' she said finally lifting her face, her adoring gaze mirroring his own. 'If this lift fell I would die the happiest woman on earth.'

'Sweetheart, if this lift fell, it would land about two floors down and you would probably be the happiest woman on earth with a broken leg.'

'Of course, I could always use you to cushion my fall.'

'Oh, could you, now?'

'You would do that for me, wouldn't you?'

'That depends.'

'On what?'

'On my prize for being such a hero.'

And then Romy grinned, ear to ear, revealing a set of dainty white teeth, before plunging towards him, ravishing him with a kiss so passionate it was all he could do to keep them both upright, his weakened knees so threatening to give way under her unbelievable barrage of intoxicating kisses.

Romy felt like crying and laughing all at once as she revelled in being in Sebastian's strong arms. Every moment became the best she had ever experienced. She grinned as tears of joy ran down her face and became one more glorious sensation of the heady kiss. And one last thought drifted into her mind before all thought was lost to the occasion.

The fates had bewitched her into loving that rickety old lift, knowing it would come in handy one day, and they had been dead right!

EPILOGUE

ROMY ran along the beach, her hair flying behind her in a tangled mess.

'Come on, Grisham!'

Her voice was captured by the salty wind and carried to the Labra-doodle bounding along way behind her. She ran up the wooden steps, two at a time. Her husband was waiting for her at their beach house and two steps at a time did not feel quick enough.

Sebastian met her on the private front porch, wearing nothing but a towel, his hair wet from his recent shower. 'How's my favourite lawyer this morning?'

'Wishing she didn't have to go back to work in a week,' Romy grumbled, pressing her cool, sand-streaked body against his clean torso.

Sebastian raised his eyebrows in disbelief.

'OK. Wishing she could stay here forever and still be the youngest partner in the Archer Law Firm's history.'

Romy grinned as she nuzzled Sebastian's warm neck. It still felt amazing to say it aloud, even after all this time.

'Though she would have been happier still if you had held off your shower until she was around to enjoy it.'

'I'll go another round if you'll join me,' Sebastian offered.

Romy scrunched up her nose. 'But won't you get all pruney? I don't know if I could bear to live with someone pruney. Not yet anyway. Maybe fifty years from now when we're both that way…'

'Mmm.' Sebastian ran a trail of hot kisses down Romy's neck. 'I'm just glad to know you'll still be here in fifty years. With me.'

'And fifty more after that if I get the chance.'

But before Romy could prove it, a tiny, bouncing version of herself tumbled out of the sand-dunes with her hands holding tight to Grisham's coat.

'Alice! Now, where did you come from?'

'Daddy sent me to get Grisham,' she said, her voice an adorable, lilting lisp.

'Did he, now?'

'Mmm,' Sebastian cooed, keeping a tight hold of his wife. 'Daddy was missing Grisham.'

'I can tell. Take Grisham inside, Alice, and I'll make you a batch of Nanna's ginger snaps.'

'Yay!' Alice cried, dragging the patient dog along behind her.

As they followed their beloved daughter into the house, Sebastian raised his head to look deep into Romy's eyes. 'Do you remember asking me once why I thought I was put here on earth?'

'Mmm.' He could feel Romy's smile as she laid soft, tantalising kisses at the edge of his mouth. 'You couldn't find a real answer.'

He gently pulled her away from her task so he could finish what he needed to say. 'I have an answer now.'

'You do?' Her eyes were heavy with desire and it took all of his strength to hold her from him. 'What is it?'

'I was put here on earth for you.'

Romy opened her eyes and pulled away, all the better to look deep into his. 'Sounds like a perfectly noble reason to me.'

'It's simple really. As you said, you were put on the earth to put order to chaos…'

'And what better example of chaos did I ever meet than you?' Romy asked, the last piece of the puzzle slipping easily into place to create the beautiful, colourful whole.

'Exactly. I was in chaos and you were my calm. I was put on this earth to find you and you were put here to find me.'

She watched him through eyes shimmering with unshed tears. 'I love that.'

'And I love you.'

Romy wrapped her arms around him until he could no longer tell where he ended and she began. And all was as it was destined to be.